# PRESSED FOR TIME OF THE THIRD PART

by

Wessall Patrick Longlly

**DORRANCE PUBLISHING CO., INC.**
PITTSBURGH, PENNSYLVANIA 15222

*Disclaimer:*

*This story is the result of a fifteen-year study of the unpublished manuscript "Pressed for Time" by William Brian Jennings.*

*Some events, names, and dates have been altered for the protection of individuals who may still be involved in a criminal enterprise, still incarcerated and under federal jurisdiction, or may have achieved elected office or appointment to a government position.*

*The reader is individually responsible for any conclusions as a result of this manuscript and advised to use discretion when sharing your ideas and thoughts with others. The only intent of the author is to inspire thought while providing entertainment.*

Please note this book has been edited and typeset in a manner to preserve the original style and intent of the author.

The opinions expressed herein are not necessarily those of the publisher or its agents.

Published for I.A.S. Productions

ISBN # 0-8059-6479-7
Printed in the United States of America

*First Printing*

For information or to order additional books, please write:
Dorrance Publishing Co., Inc.
701 Smithfield Street
Third Floor
Pittsburgh, Pennsylvania 15222
U.S.A.
1-800-788-7654
Or visit our web site and on-line catalog at www.dorrancepublishing.com

### *Special Dedications and Thanks:*

*To my mother, who always gave unconditional love with her advice and direction.*

*To my father, who taught me the values that kept me alive long enough to know he was right.*

*To my children, who give me unconditional love and so many grand- children.*

*To every girl I ever kissed, and every woman I ever loved forever.*

*To Paul Ashley, attorney at law, your plan may have been a better one for me.*

*To the cast and crew of the {LBF}, "In Heat," for sharing your world with me.*

*To Melissa Z.L.—I finally took your advice, now I need some more.*

*To Rose N. and Mrs. A for scolding me for striving for less than my ability.*

*To the lovely Mrs. Denton, who inspired me with her courage and her encouragement.*

*To Solange Solange, I am not sorry I took the train. It made for a story we both may tell!*

# Introduction

*I would have never thought that a walk down a tiny road to a dump that is closed would net me such a reward! The stranger came out of nowhere! Something deep inside of me had always known that I would meet this stranger somewhere sometime in my future. His old green Chevy pick-up truck jiggled and shook as it idled at the side of the road.*

*He asked me where it was that I thought I was going. My reply was that I did not know.*

"That's when the adventure begins," *the stranger began to say.* "For when a man goes off half-cocked, he should expect to get half-screwed!"

*As it turned out, this stranger was very much like myself!*

*Jump in, he gestured with his big hand and arm.* "I will take you on a journey to where I have already been."

**Then the *stranger continued,*** "I remember thinking once that it must be against the law! *Shush click, shush click*—that's the sound of a finely tuned offset printing press. *Shush click* as sheets of hundred dollar bills fell gently to rest in the soft stack of the receiving tray. Six bills to a sheet, the press is running at slow speed! Five thousand sheets an hour, five times through the press and presto! Four hundred and eighty-five dollars worth of paper is transformed into a little over ten million dollars!"

*I could not help myself. I had to ask, "How little over ten million was it?"*

"I don't know," he continued. "Probably closer to just under fifteen million, if you count the two and a half-million in fifties that were never found. Only a brand new unused set of plates for the fifties was ever recovered by the Secret Service!"

*"So you were busted and did time?"*

"Twice; once is never enough! You cannot just counterfeit once! That would be like just having sex once! If you knew what I was talking about then you would know that sex is a damn good metaphor for counterfeiting! It's such a rush; I had a heart attack both times! I was not even forty yet and I have a good strong heart even today, but that does not change the facts!"

*"You got any regrets about that whole thing now that it is all behind you!"*

"Regrets, I've got a few! That's a song title or should be. Yeah, I regret missing those years with my children! Ten years in the life of a child is damn well over fifty percent, but I cannot change that! The lies of the English language. There is no making up for or starting over. Life is linear; it goes forward, and over begins at death."

*Again, I spoke out of turn. "Any other regrets for things you could have done differently?"*

"I almost think that I should have done it just one more time! My dad said it first! It blew me away when he said it. I was in the new federal joint in Tucson, Arizona. Mom and Dad had driven in from Quartszite for a weekend visit. They had visited Saturday and Sunday they would leave early to drive back to Quartszite. Mom excused herself and went to the bathroom. Dad leaned in across the table. He was as serious as a heart attack when he said, 'Only one way you can ever get even with them for this'. I leaned in close to hear what he was going to say next. I already could not believe what I was hearing. I was led to believe that John Birch was my daddy's first cousin. So I never expected him to say, 'Do it again and not get caught'! My oldest brother said that my only problem in life is that I never picked just one thing and stuck with it. My girlfriend wants to break up just so we can get back together again. She says the third time's the charm! I know one thing for sure—I never needed a partner. I will never have a partner in crime again!"

# CHAPTER ONE
## IN THE FIRST PART

*It was just like I said before*—it was the *shush click*; the sweetest, sexiest sound in the world, the sound of a machine making money. However that's not how it started! You just don't decide to be a counterfeiter, or at least I didn't.

I was probably about eight when I hoisted myself up on the edge of the kitchen sink to a glass of water. From there, I could see out the window, across the field that was our farm. My dad was walking a garden tractor up and down the rows he was cultivating. He had already worked eight hours at the Quincy naval shipyard. That did not count the two hours of travel time. It was the '50s and the world had a clean, fresh feeling to it, like a virgin just before the senior prom.

I remember being poised there on my belly, holding myself suspended above the floor with the help of the cold water faucet. My dad had to work too damn hard for the little bit he seemed to get, while all around me I saw that there were those who had obviously found another way. Then they made how they got there disappear. At least that's the way it seemed to me at age eight.

I spent my whole life looking for the back door to wealth and happiness, just to find out it's out front right where you can see it! Moreover, if you could see who goes through that other front door, what choices would you have made differently?

My older sister and my two older brothers turned out totally different, honest and prosperous. Hard for some folks to figure how we came from the same gene strand, if it were not for the fact that I'm a blueprint copy of my dad in both looks and frame. It's even scarier when you take note that my youngest child is a son and is also a blueprint of me. The only thing I can say to that is I did not follow in my father's footsteps and I pray to God that he does not follow mine—at least not the first fifty years' worth.

Let us not forget that if you are looking for a back door, you will find it. I did, many times. It was a scam; they all were. That's what I did for a living—

a locator and franchise salesman! People ask me all the time if I feel guilty about my past. I feel guilty about being a locator and franchise salesman.

My mentor the last flim-flam man, and he taught me. Joe could make jumping off Niagara Falls look like it was a good idea and paying him for it would be a sound investment.

Instant printing was all the rage! Economists claimed that in five years every man, woman, and child in America would consume 850 pounds of printed material a year, not counting dated publications. Me and the flim-flam man put together a little plan, a franchisable package with opportunity written all over it and my passport to destiny!

Growing up back east, on the Cape, in old Massachusetts, the land from whence all old sayings came from when opportunity knocks. Where in hell are the directions to that? What good is all that information if you do not provide instruction? My mother always said, whenever I would stray from the straight and narrow, "Oh what a tangled web we weave, when once we practice to deceive!" Is this not somehow connected to "Practice makes perfect?" For me it seems my opportunities all knock at the back door!

This opportunity provided me with a two-year crash course in lithography. The instructors would give me the two-year course in lithography and I would change it into a six-week instant printing training program for that new industry, most specifically our franchise package. Joe had worked out a little deal with the school. Everybody got what they wanted out of the deal. The school got a class they could sell to a new big market, and we did not have to spend a dime on our new owner's training program until we sold a unit.

We had eight weeks to get it all done. So I went to Louiston Auburn Trade Tech. I was truly inspired, learning at a speed that gave my instructors the feeling they were learning from me. It was like being born to it. Some part of destiny had found me, of that I was sure! If destiny is the result of life being lived, then I was right—destiny had found me.

I insisted that our franchise package included a "dark room camera." If you are going to make perfect copies, you need to start with a perfect negative. Unfortunately, I did not achieve that perfect negative until the second time I crawled through the back door.

Louiston Auburn Trade Tech was like a prep school. Federal prison was the university, if university means a place where you get a "real education!" Federal prison was my university.

*"FPU—they should have t-shirts. How about FPI of C (Federal Prison Institute of Conspiracy)? You could get a Ph.D. in criminology if you were there long enough!"*

Federal prison is where you find all those famous ones who did not succeed in covering their tracks. The feds were using electronic devices, redefining privacy, and changing the rules of justice. There was a time in America when just getting across the state line meant you were home free. Whatever happened to the sanctity of statehood? That and marijuana both on the same day. Kind of makes you wonder what the real reason was they took away the protection of statehood.

The second time was going to be much harder. I had learned things they do not teach at other universities. You know, opportunity knocked again and I said, "Let me get it. It's the back door, so it must be for me."

***Knock, knock***. Who's there? Bogart, your future crime partner, and I have a little book here from that place in Bolder, Colorado, titled: *Everything the Secret Service Knows about Counterfeit and Counterfeit Operations.*

I was just lounging there on my bunk with an open window blowing a warm summer breeze across the top of a genetically created bald spot. This was not the first time Bogart the ex-Bank of America yacht broker and I had discussed the replication of transactional certificates. I first met Bogart on Front Street. No, that is a real place and the feds thought it would be fun to put a prison on it, the palatial downtown "Metropolitan Correctional Center." I do not know how tall it was, just that I was on the twelfth floor, downtown San Diego. Semi-private rooms and an impressive guest list, starting with Christopher Boyce, known to the media and the rest of the world as the Falcon. He looked more like my brother Jim than my brother did. Looking back, I wonder, Was it just by chance? With at least eleven other floors, what are the odds that Bogart, the yacht broker banker; Crazy Bobby, the funniest bank robber I ever met; Big Joe, the speed boss; Boyce, international spy; and this salesman/counterfeiter from the small town of Carver, Massachusetts, all ended up roommates, cellies, homeboys, road dogs, or time travelers into the future?

Nothing at the time seemed any stranger than me being there. I was not a convict, I felt like nothing in my life had been preparation for this. I was wrong—being a locator and franchise salesman had taught me how to create a facade. I would simply become the inmate. It must have worked, because I always ran with the "big dogs" and I never pretended to be anything but what I was, the counterfeiter. Seems I'm not the only one who gets off on recycling paper for profit.

*"We had driven all night into the barren landscape of the high desert above Palm Springs. The sun rising red as blood in the east, twilight giving way to a new day. Red sun in the morning, sailors take warning! I was just beginning see the things I had never seen before."*

Bogart wanted to know if the book was any good, the stranger continued. I fanned through it two or three times. "How could it be any good? It's seventy-five pages, half of them bad pictures."

3

"Can you get anything from it of value?" Bogart's whole demeanor was begging for a response.

"I don't know. I'll look at it. Now get out of here. You're ruining a good Saturday high here at Club Fed!"

As soon as Bogart was gone, I began to skim through it. Bogart did not like my friends much and I preferred their friendship and company more than I like hanging with him. He had a dark soul, it seemed to me.

The whole idea was ludicrous. From the dollar seventy-five price stamp to the ridiculous claim that it was everything that they knew about something that had been going on since before Christ was born. And all they got was seventy-five pages! Yeah, I was impressed! I was also wrong! The title should have been "Everything You Do Not Already Know about Counterfeiting," Or perhaps "The Counterfeiters Handbook." I cannot honestly say that everyone would have found the information in those seventy-five pages as valuable as I did, but then this was not everyone's destiny.

Bogart and I already had a plan. I would produce the counterfeit; Bogart would supply the front money and roll over the counterfeit. After all, he was the banker, and I was this undefinable entity, half-human and half-machine that made money.

It's not too early to introduce the phenomenon I like to call the "Counterfeit Freekies." Imagine for a moment that you have a friend who has some equipment, and when you put the friend and the equipment together you have a money-making machine. How much money is enough? When would you want to turn your money-making machine off, permanently? Do you really want to be the counterfeiter?

Welcome to the Counterfeit Freekies! You definitely do not want to be the counterfeiter. There is just no future in being a money-making machine that does not make money anymore.

The things I changed in the plan as a result of reading the book did not make Bogart happy. It went something like this:

"If it is going to take longer and cost more money, do we really need to change the plan? That just does not make any sense to me," Bogart reasoned.

"How about increasing the street life of the bills to infinity instead of two to three weeks? Does that make sense to you, Bogie? More importantly, just by changing one-third of the printing plates, we get another eighteen thousand series numbers for another ten million dollars of twenties, fifties, and hundreds."

"What does that come out to on my end?" Bogart was anxiously waiting for the big dollar sign to fall out of the sky.

"Every bill in a million dollars will have a different series number. Every million will be one-third twenties, one-third fifties, and one-third hundreds.

There will be an equal amount of each of eleven different mint codes; the eleventh mint code will be doubled to make it come out even, making it the same as twelve mint codes instead of eleven."

"So we can put everything in storage, just in case we want another ten million dollars!" Bogart had enough juice in his mouth to drool.

I had not missed the fact that he said "want," not "need," another ten million dollars. I imagine women know what it feels like to be looked upon as property. Bogart was a banker; there were only two things he understood: performing assets and non-performing assets. I was about to become a performing asset. The fact we were friends seemed more in his favor than mine.

I was almost finished with my first sentence. My wife had moved away and was divorcing me for the second time, even though we had only been married once. The United States Navy court-martialed me out of the service. That was not as bad as it sounded. I received a general discharge under honorable conditions. I turned a hanging into a five-day vacation from prison and met a young, beautiful girl from Switzerland and at only eighteen, she was the most sophisticated woman I had ever met. I know what you are thinking, but you are wrong. Future events will prove a different truth.

*The stranger chuckled smugly as if there was an untold secret that I awaited the answer to.*

It was destiny and destiny is never wrong! I, on the other hand, already had a plan, a partner, and funding for the largest, most sophisticated counterfeit operation ever in the United States.

I had a brand new girlfriend! Redheads, real or counterfeit, are bad luck just waiting for someone like me to come along. I had a red Ford pick-up once, nothing but trouble. I had a red sailboat, 'til it sank! I had a redheaded ex-wife who divorced me twice.

While I was at Lompoc doing time, when I wasn't smuggling booze, drugs, and marijuana onto the compound or helping Chris perform one of the most successful escapes in that prison's history, five of us camp inmates would be off in a prison car or van, lecturing to school kids and troubled teens in the Santa Barbara County School District. You see, the only thing I knew about being confined by anal-retentive prison wardens I'd learned from the old black and white TV series "Hogan's Heroes." Nobody told me that it was not real. It seemed real enough to me when I used the prison pick-up to make bank deposits for myself and several other inmates every Tuesday at 9:30 A.M.

One time it did seem unreal. Ernie and I were up on the edge of the prison property gathering wood for a barbecue for our maximum-security friends, two inmates with chainsaws in the woods between the federal prison and Vandenburg Air Base. I had been wood gathering in these woods before and had plans for the whole day. We had the cooler stuffed with food and beverages. Not just beer, Miller's in bottles, not cans. After all, they do say, "If you got the time, we've got the beer." Hell, I had four years—how much time you got to have? We had some excellent herb and a good radio playing my favorite songs. "Coke-a-Cola Cowboy" was one of my favorites at the time. Hey, I was doing time. Don't expect me to have class, too.

We had busted ass all morning and loaded the tractor's utility trailer to overflowing. Then we broke for lunch. After what seemed like an eternity of thought I began to wander around. I quite literally stumbled on to this huge gully. Like a small canyon, it was about twenty feet deep and crammed with vegetation growing up from the valley floor and towering over the upper ridge.

I called to Ernie and together we descended into this eco-world with giant ferns and other plants that one would have never expected to see here in this otherwise bleak landscape. If we had not been hammered, we probably would not have believed our eyes. Like a childhood imaginary world from before time. The sandstone walls of the canyon seeped with trickles of water. The floor was covered with more than eighteen inches of mulch and held moisture enough to survive anything, including a full on drought.

It was decided we would return the next day and spread every seed we could lay our hands on. We both got to feel firsthand the thrill that Johnny Appleseed must have felt when he planted all those trees.

It was on a lecture date that I met the counterfeit redhead! Teri and her friend Wendy were driving school busses for the county. Bill, my co-speaker, and I were just stepping out of the restroom after toking up at the new Santa Barbara County Library. Teri and Wendy were walking away! Tight jeans with hair down their backs as soft and shiny as spun gold. They must have heard the sound of blood pumping through restricted veins, because they turned around and gave us a tiny wave.

"We'll be back; we just have to go get some more kids," they said with coy voices.

Three or four members of Seven Steps and myself as president had been speaking to the kids in these schools for almost a year. The school district loved us and we were getting a lot of coverage from Channel Seven Eyewitness News. The head of the school district knew the Federal Bureau of Prisons was trying to shut us down because we were so popular. Therefore, the district supervisor decided that before that happened he would put on one massive performance. He would bring together all the kids who had a police record, or a brother, sister, mother, or father doing time. Two hundred and fifty students, plus teachers, faculty, and several federal agents came to this grand farewell appearance of our little group.

The auditorium sounded like a sports bar during Monday Night Football. The district supervisor tried several times to get the kids to quiet down. Finally he handed the mic off to me and said, "Good luck!"

Teri and Wendy were right down in the front row. I started to walk back and forth in front of the stage. I was ready, I was pumped, and I was calm and comfortable as I began to speak. For the next two hours, the only sound in that room was the sound of us speaking the truth about what the life of a criminal was all about. We fielded questions for about another half-hour. Then we mingled, hand to hand, heart to heart. These children wanted answers. They knew the answers we gave them were real. We were the proof that could not lie to them.

The students figured out that Teri and I needed some quality time, so they kind of ran cover for us. I gave her my address. Then she tried to give me hers. I told her I didn't need her address unless it was on her letter. That's how I got a sexy redheaded girlfriend in tight jeans and a full deck while I was still in prison.

This time I was going to do it right. The right equipment, the right paper, and the right information. All I had to figure out was how I was going to juggle all of the many different me's there were going have to be. While one of me created the first ten million dollars, the other me was a working cattle broker, boyfriend to Teri in Santa Barbara, the salesman absentee father of my children and ex-wife in Paradise, California, and the new businessman in the little towns of Beaumont and Banning, just west of Palm Springs.

I had acted before, so many times, so many roles, so many places, but the lines never change and the outcome was what we call the *scam*.

We finally settled in Beaumont after Bogart brought unnecessary heat on two other locations in Palm Springs. I had rented a nice fully furnished three-bedroom home with swimming pool and hot tub. I convinced the real estate broker that I was a used heavy equipment speculator, that I was going through a sticky divorce and would be paying cash, and she assured me that there would be no credit check for my wife's attorney to trace.

Now we're in a storage unit on the corner of Orange and 5th Street in Beaumont, California. Everybody in town knows all about me. I'm a charity broker. I supply non-profit organizations with re-saleable merchandise for fundraisers. I had the spiel and the samples to prove it.

Whenever I would have to leave my little business for more then twenty-four hours, the entire neighborhood would watch over my stuff, including the local police department. I told you I was the last flim-flam man.

Before I would leave, I would give away two or three boxes of candy bars to the kids, cigarettes to the young hoodlums, and one or two cases of beer to the neighborhood fathers.

I appeared to be one of the wealthiest single men in the area, with a brand new Cougar XR-7. I generously tipped everyone in town, from the car wash to the hair salon, even the raven-haired girl at the drive-through dairy. Redheads will set you on fire and what is left a raven-haired woman will turn to embers 'til all that is left is dust. It takes a long time before a fire like that dies out! Of course, you also have to take into account that she was Indian, German, and Irish. "Hot" would be an understatement.

Life was good in Beaumont. I relaxed. The things that had not worked suddenly worked perfectly. I remember it just like it was yesterday. My local girlfriend was having a bad day. I had just barely gotten the new shop up and running. I'd just set the camera up for some color separation and the first two test shots did not prove out. Jane stopped by with her twin little blonde boys in her boyfriend's old wreck of a car. Jane was mostly Native American with some Mexican mixed in, but you could still tell who the mother was in the faces of those little fair-haired boys. So I decided that we should all take the day off and go to Knotts Berry Farm. It was a great day and that night her sister watched the boys and Jane spent the night with me.

The next morning I was getting a later than normal start on the day. I was busy playing catch up when I reset the camera. As I had no luck dropping the black out of the green with the B-54 filter, I slipped in the G-45 filter to drop the green out of the black. I gave it a little longer exposure time than I had used the morning before. I set up the tanks and developed the negative. Nothing—just solid black like it had not even been exposed to light. Rather than puzzle over it, I doubled the exposure time to seventy-five seconds. Still the negative was underexposed, however there was a curious-looking spot on the negative. That's when I realized that I had not taken the first filter out. Once again, I looked at the curious spot on the negative. It was at 156 seconds that I created the most perfect negative ever made from a circulated bill. Before the day was over, I had fifty-six perfect plates of the front and back of the twenty, fifty, and hundred dollar bills.

I had not forgotten to enlarge the PMT shots by 4.4 percent! I can thank the book for that one. My mother always told me the more you read, the more you'll know. Stay in school. Illiterate children do not make sophisticated criminals.

I had decided not to tell Bogart of my successes! From now on I was keeping my progress reports three days in arrears. As Bogart was now too paranoid to actually come to the print shop. He was so freaked after having to leave Palm Springs that he would not even drive by the shop or honk so I'd know he was in town.

This was the result of a falling out between Bogart and myself. It went as far as trying to dissolve the partnership. I had traveled all the way back to New Hampshire in an attempt to sell off my end of the deal.

When I returned Bogart informed me of the new deal. I had just lowered my head to one of the glass shelves that separated the kitchen from the dining room and took a line of cocaine up my nose. Bogart went to the far side of the round glass dining room table. When I turned to face him, he popped the latches of his briefcase as it lay on the table in front of him. He raised the lid just enough to remove a western Colt revolver that would be proudly displayed in any gun worshiper's cabinet. As he raised it to his temple, I thought that there is no such thing as free cocaine. It seems that Mr. Bogart financed his end of the deal by selling me like futures on the open market.

In his words if I did not deliver at least two million dollars within a reasonable length of time, "They are going to kill me and then they're going to fuck with your kids until you give them what they want."

Knowing Bogart the way I did, it figured he had associates twisted enough to do just that.

So I had to make a new plan. Originally my cut was the biggest ever paid for funny money, thirty-three and a third percent per ten million dollars. Teri did not know a thing about what I was doing. She knew Bogart only by his voice; she told me he was going to kill me, she could feel it. I'd been to school, I knew the rules. I had known for sometime that it was going to be the only way this partnership was going to end. Bogart knew it from the get-go, he was the professional. I was just a beginner! He was going to have to kill me before I figured it out, but not before I delivered the goods.

It was still Bogart's job to do the shopping! I told him I needed a gun. Bogart told me he would get me a gun. That same day I drove to LA and looked up an old friend of mine known as Eddie the Grip, the youngest man ever elected to the family council. I told Eddie I wanted a snubnose with clip-on holster and a safety. We sat around and talked about other times and other places. We passed the mirror and lied about what we were each doing now.

Eddie did not want to give me a gun. He offered to hit whomever it was I needed hit, no charge. Hindsight is not the same as a rearview mirror. If it's behind you, it's done. Hell, Eddie, would have paid me to let him waste Bogart. All he needed was an excuse, I don't even think it had to be a good one.

In about an hour there was a knock on the door of Eddie's LAX AirFreight office. A youngster entered the room and placed a small brown paper bag on Eddie's desk. "Is it what I asked for?" Eddie said, trying to act up to his reputation of the mean old tough Mafia gangster.

Young blood stuck out his hand and said, "Not until you pay for it, it ain't nothin'!"

Eddie jammed a hundred-dollar bill in his hand with a couple of ten mil bottles of pure Columbia's finest! When Young blood turned and started for the door, he shot me a grin and a wink. It seemed I knew him from the yard at Lompoc. He was the one who always got me what I needed in the joint. It was a perfect fit with the western grip and a safety. I just can't bring myself to jam a loaded pistol down my pants without a safety. When I hooked the holster clip to the inside of the back of my pants, I sat down with my back squarely against the back of the chair. It felt perfect. I am not sure I should tell you that it felt as if a hot sexy woman had just caressed my thigh. I slid the box of special loads into my slick black leather jacket pocket and stood to leave.

"That's it. You got the gun; see ya later. This is the way you treat your friends? Come on, sit down relax. We go to dinner, stop by the club, get a couple of girls. Virginia is back working at Big Mac's club the Rocket. Seems to me you liked her once. You could maybe like her again."

The difference between a traveling salesman and a criminal is the style and class of the woman they get to sleep with, even though I did not do too badly as a traveling salesman.

"Give my respects to the big man. I can't stay. I'm really pressed for time. Give me a couple of weeks on that raincheck and I'll have a business deal for you and the big man!"

"You're handling this wrong, Trash, whatever it is. Word is you are back in the trash business. I could pick up all of your paper. I'll beat anybody's money without even lookin' at it."

I grabbed the doorknob and turned to face him as I opened the door. "Sorry, Zuba, I'm just at a place I can't turn around in. You'll hear from me when I can."

Bogart owned me; I was not going to make the same mistake with the grip or Big Mac. I will clean up my own mess and take back my life or be better off dead.

I was back in Beaumont in time to meet Bogart at my motel. I had takeout food when I drove up so Bogart never got the idea that I had not remained in Beaumont all day while he was in Anaheim purchasing an electric bench top paper cutter with a spare blade. He apologized for not being able to get a gun, but he would keep trying. He assured me he would get me one by the time the money was ready. I told him that was not good enough. I wanted one now, in case one of the people he sold me off to comes looking for a bigger share. He would not explain why I did not need to worry about that.

It was not my theory, it was Nixon's. If you want to pull off the big scam, you're going to need some really crooked gangsters! Bogart was a crooked gangster. Predestination or self-destruction? I was still working on how I was going to get out of this alive and keep my children safe. Then if there was any way I could end up with just a little something for my efforts, that would be a bonus. Oh, I forgot to tell you, Bogart was a real redhead, with freckles, a ruddy complexion, and a big brush mustache. He looked the part of a crooked banker.

Before Bogie left, I put bait on his hook. I told him that I expected to be done cutting the last stack of paper on a run of two million in twenties and hundreds within two weeks from right now—if everything continued to go as scheduled, I added just as a precaution. Bogart was pissed it was not all hundreds. The fifty did not make the cut, I told him. Besides the new deal was two million. They should be happy it's not fives, the easiest bill to counterfeit. I then told him where to go and buy six cases of Crowns Distaff Linen Bond Certificate Stock as we had already wasted ten cases of stock that had been cut wrong. The watermark was all over the place. The ten million of hundreds were almost useless. Between the plates being flawed, the negatives were poor compared to my latest efforts and the watermark was everywhere it should not be. We wouldn't net ten percent, and they still had not been numbered.

"Why didn't you say anything this morning before I left for Anaheim?" Bogart scorned.

"I did not know until I finished up today. Besides, it wouldn't have changed anything. The paper is in LA, and the cutter had to be picked up today in Anaheim."

"It's just if you had the paper today, you could be printing tomorrow!"

"Slow it down, Bogart, I have to make over fifty plates. I need the paper soon but it won't be tomorrow. It could be as soon as the day after that."

It was a plan. Bogart would come by in the morning, we would go do breakfast, and I would give him a note with detailed information—who to see, what to buy, and accept no substitutes. As soon as he left, I would head over to Riverside and pick up four cases of the same paper that Bogart was buying in LA.

*"I do not understand; how much paper do you need to print two million dollars?"*

"I told you I had a new plan. The time it takes to print ten million is not even notable over the time it takes to print two million." The time was in the 256 plate changes. Bogart wouldn't kill me before the job is done. Bogart won't know when the job is done until I tell him. He had not figured out that with eighteen thousand different serial numbers on twenties, fifties, and hundreds, I did not need to do laundry. Use it just like cash anywhere, even the bank. By the time another one with the same numbers showed up, you're done and gone. The trump card is Bogart is under the impression that I still do not have a gun.

On the way back from Riverside, I will check out a place where I can take out Bogart and leave him in the trunk of his own car. In a day or two, the buzzards will have eaten the Landau top off his Lincoln Town Car looking for his rotten carcass.

"The feds could have him back. I had also figured it so that the people who hold my mortgage get the value Bogart promised. They would also understand I'm not for sale. If you endanger my family, you die. That goes double for federal agents.

*Isn't that a little extreme, killing a man just because he tried to forced you to do business with him?*

Putting a price tag on my family was not the way to insure loyalty. That and the fact that he recklessly brought heat on what was ultimately a hundred million dollar counterfeit operation over a pennyante coke deal was reason enough to kill him. Didn't Forest Gump teach us "Stupid is and stupid dies first!"

***What ever happened to that small town farm boy from Carver, Massachusetts?***

# CHAPTER TWO

*Just like in* politics, big business, and sports, the more digits before the decimal point, the rougher the game! I wondered what it was that I had created of myself, a federal prisoner, or an outlaw? All I can say to that is, destiny has already spoken!

On the way back from Riverside, I choreographed every move I would make when I took Bogart out. The location was perfect. Now you know the definition of premeditated murder.

Bogart would feel very comfortable knowing how secluded our rendezvous is. I will give him a chance to check it out in advance. I parked my car behind the hill and walked back out to the highway. The whole area was completely obscured by the curve of the little hill and the road that turned away, just up the road from the county dump.

Bogart and his lame-witted partner Ed would be out of my life. With my note, holders compensated by the time the smell or the buzzards give him up, I will be southbound with about two million in fifties and hundreds. I know someone in Costa Rica who can sell me what I need for a whole lot less than what I have.

I arrived back in Beaumont with time enough to drop off the two cases of paper and the ten new wooden paper presses. After you wash cloth you must press it or it will wrinkle. Certificate stock is 80 percent linen and 20 percent cotton, just like money. Then they coat it with wood pulp to give it body. So you may produce certificates, no matter how you slice it. It is controlled paper but not unattainable in small quantities.

I discovered it not more than a year before my life went from cruise to race. I was working for a small publishing house in Hampshire, Illinois. I stepped out the shop door looking for our delivery boy to show up. Paper scraps were blowing out of the Dumpster. I closed the lid, and picked up a single strip of paper. It was about a half-inch wide and eight and a half-inches long. Half of it was submerged in water, the other end was propped up against the steel wheel of the Dumpster. I keep coming back to destiny.

I squeezed off the wet end by pulling it between my thumb and forefinger two or three times before tossing it on the end table of the automated paper cutter. About an hour later, I found it on the floor by the paper cutter's footbrake. The wet end had dried and wrinkled, it also looked and felt much different. I pride myself for being able to identify paper by touch. I noticed little red and blue fibers on the washed end. I grabbed my micrometer from my back pocket and measured the thickness of the washed end. With my hands full of stuff I did not want to set down, I scrambled for my wallet and extracted a twenty-dollar bill and I mic'ed the non-image area. Then like a crazed shopper I scanned the shelves for the name of that paper. Then I went to that area of my brain marked "memory" and punched enter.

When I was at Lompoc Federal Prison, one of my many jobs was to keep the administration's printing press up and running. However that was only in emergencies. So while I was fulfilling a little emergency, I conducted some paper washing experiments. One of them worked!

I told Bogart that I was going to work most of the night so I could stay on schedule. That inspired him to drop off the paper and some expense money without his usual long list of questions. Instead he said nothing and just left, no doubt feeling guilty because he knew he had to kill me, he knew the rules. He knew it was soon!

Back inside my world, things were clicking. Washing the paper was a long, tedious task. In spite of its tedious pace, I could not help feeling exhilarated. I changed the drive pulley set-up on the AB Dick 360 to slow it way down to hand-crank speed. The brand new special service moliton roller covers were carrying the maximum amount of my specially formulated detergent and wetting agent, a mixture of Amway, water, Liquid Wisk, and transferring it to the plate cylinder. I had made a set of peeling fingers out of a sheet of copper to peel the wet paper off of the drum should they become stuck. I installed a clip-on blow dryer in front of the fingers to blow the leading edge of the paper and start the drying process. Never had boredom been so exciting. I fanned the wet stock out all over the workbenches. This would not be easy to explain if someone was to show up uninvited!

As soon as the paper was almost dry from the first run, I ran them through again. I was still cutting the wax paper eight and a half-inches long by its roll width, making it an inch longer than the paper. So as the paper came out of the press from the second time, it became a simple process of one piece of wax paper, one piece of rag paper. Once a paper press was full, the top was put on with a good degree of pressure to ensure they turned out crisp and flat, most likely explaining why money was referred to as lettuce by both con and gangster. By about half-past breakfast time, I'd washed and pressed fifty thousand sheets of paper. Now all there was to do was shut the pump off on the evaporative cooler and keep the blower on high. That and the late summer sun on the black hot-top roof should get the job done so I can start printing tonight.

Right now, it was breakfast time, and the only problem I had was between Beaumont and Banning, there were at least twenty places you could get eggs and a short stack to die for. Today, though, it was going to be Louie's. It was not the best. However I could see the print shop door and the dark-haired ultras opening up the drive-through dairy from my booth in the window of Louie's Diner.

Once is never enough for many things in life. Being burnt right down to your socks was one of them. Making money paper is just as erotic as the printing of it. I highly recommend that you just take my word on that!

After making a non-committal date for the not-too-certain future with the waitress, I went back to the print shop and took a shower. Then I crashed on the cold concrete floor. I woke up about two in the afternoon, just long enough to eat. Then I turned the pump back on and went to sleep on the old army cot until seven-thirty. I put my car on the apron out front like I had gone off with someone or just took a walk, like I had in the past.

The windows were blacked out at night so no light leaked out. The radio ran night and day, twenty-four and seven, whether I was there or not. The only thing you could hear from outside was country music, even when the press was running.

It was time to put theory to the test. First I had some real tedious manual labor to perform. I pulled the first crib apart, laying one piece of paper on the bench, and swept it on both sides with a long thin wallpaper brush. My magic soap naturalized the bonding agents that allowed the wood pulp to bond with the linen. It had dried up into billions of micro-sized spitballs. Fifty thousand times I would repeat this process while slipping a piece of colored paper into the stack every two hundred and fifty sheets. The single colored sheet was a visual aid to tell me when to change to the next plate. It was also the recommended cutting depths for the paper cutter. It would cut down operating time by more than ten hours.

Prison affords you the time to get anal about every detail of your crime. A very wise woman would come to tell me one day, "It's your time, use it wisely, and obtain wisdom!"

Where is the part-time help for counterfeiters? What would the ad in the paper read like? "Must be self-motivated, could turn into a career, with room and board paid for by the feds. Apply at the rear door of Slim's Print Shop. Make sure you're not followed."

I needed to organize the printing plates in the order they will be used. Each front and back for each mint code meant twelve stacks of paper, with a piece of colored paper every two hundred and fifty sheets. So as soon as the first five thousand sheets of paper were ready, I changed the pulley on the press and put the drive pulley back on. As I was going to do the J Series twice, I decided to use the first set of J Series plates for the first run of twenties, fifties, and hundreds.

*You double up on the J Series because your last name begins with a J?*

If only that were true, I would call it vanity. If it were not destiny, would it have turned out any less than perfect? That's about the first time in my life that I was really scared. Just looking at the first couple of pulls off a super-clean press sent a chill. It was about six-thirty in the morning when I looked down and saw the green backs of three one hundred-dollar bills going *shushs click*! That thing was happening again! This time I was ready for it. I laid down flat on my back, reached in my shirt pocket, and took a hammer-size hit off of a half-smoked doobie. Faster than nitro, with no harmful side effects, and I was back on my feet enjoying the euphoria of my victory and my accomplishments.

Key players are targets in politics, big business, and specialized crime. The quality of these bills made me a key player. Little did I know what it was that really made me a key player. What was it you said, Mom? Something about a tangled web and deception? The rest of that day I kept on smoking the marijuana, just to keep the hypertension at a level my heart could handle. This was going to work! These bills will fly!

By nine P.M. I needed to be unplugged. I knew of this one really cute double for Sissy Spacek! Her old man was a falling down out of work drunk most of the time. I drove him and her home the first night I met her at JR's. We shoved his drunken butt out on somebody else's front lawn on the other side of town and we went off to have a party of our own. I think maybe if I'm lucky she will be available to unplug me tonight.

As it turned out she was available. We went to the motel, and I could not function. I was totally beside myself. How can you be so emotionally turned on and not function? Was this ex-con erection syndrome or the result of prolonged intake of federal food? So I got almost no sleep. In the morning, I was really ready and she was very late for work. I had no idea how many years were going to pass before we got to make that up. I went back to the shop and slept until noon and started in again. Now the long runs were finished and now there are only two hundred more plate changes. One every two hundred and fifty sheets. Now it starts to become money, and the doobie is on the stand by!

*It comes out even!*

Of course, it came out even. Do you think I was just making up numbers? I was going to pace myself. This was not the time to rush, because we all know haste makes waste! Yeah, and then what?

You're not going to sleep now! You're not going to leave the building except to get food. You're going to call attention to yourself unless you stop living like a vampire!

The weekend was coming, ending the first of the two weeks. I would be finished cutting by the end of this weekend! Bogart came by my motel promptly and grinning from ear to ear in anticipation of what I was going to show him. As soon as he came through the door, I stuck a sheet of the backs of hundred-dollar bills under his nose with nothing printed on the other side.

"What does it look like cut out?" he asked.

I pulled one from my shirt pocket and he looked amazed when he turned it over and there was nothing on the other side.

"You want to make a little bet, Bogie?"

"Yeah, but wait a minute—I've had to piss ever since I left Palm Springs."

"Did you bring the five new hundred-dollar bills?"

"Yeah!"

"Lay them on the bed face up and then go in the bathroom and take your piss. Do not look at the backs and do not open the door until I say I'm ready."

I arranged the bills on the bed in an irregular fashion. Then I told Bogart to come out. He stood looking at the bed with fifteen bills, backside up. "Pick out your bills, Bogart. For every one you get wrong you owe me one hundred dollars." Bogart was a banker. He was sure I could not fool him. He had to keep picking until he got all five of his bills back.

Bogart left happy and owing an additional three hundred dollars! He was going to be so dead when I shoot him. I will have my hand on his shoulder and looking him square in the eye when I squeeze off the shot! My gun will be buried in his belly button! It will be loaded with one scored hollow point ready to do the job. His hand-tailored suit will muffle the sound.

• • •

*"Can you tell me anymore," I asked intently, "without incriminating yourself?"*

*"Not this way," the stranger said as he pulled the old green, Chevy pick-up truck to the edge of the narrow paved road and stopped. "The gates are locked. We cannot go any further in this direction."*

*"You must go on. I must know more."*

*"Very well, then let us take this pathway. There are no roads and there are no locked gates," he said as he turned the pick-up out into the desert.*

*The headlights jumped from side to side and up and down as we rolled slowly across the drifted sand and rocks, spotlighting an object for a moment, and then another, images frozen in time like pictures on a wall. What could this stranger tell*

*me now that I did not already know? "Am I safe? I mean, nothing is going to hap-
pen to me?" I asked, more curious than scared.*

Wouldn't it be a shame if we lived our whole life, and nothing ever happened to us or we were never in danger or took a chance? Wouldn't that be
more like not living? You already know where the straight and narrow leads.
The only sure thing in a nothing happened life is death and taxes. Death is
certain, tax is optional, and everything else in life is a chance, a chance to succeed or a chance to fail, but not unless you try. Death is not an achievement
unless you had to overcome or overwhelm something or someone of great
consequence. What are you afraid of, life or living it? If you are not living on
the edge, you do not have the best view.

# CHAPTER THREE

*It was going* to be easy now; I had already done the impossible. The cases of money were packed all the way forward in the low-boy rental trailer. The printing press was dead over the axles. The trash and odds and ends were crammed in boxes and black trash bags. Everything looking very unimportant.

Everything that could have left the mark of counterfeit was on its way to the landfill or storage. I took one more discerning look at the warehouse before I closed the door on it for the last time. The wall I put up to create a front office was gone. I had used some of it to build a ramp for the heavy equipment and build a press dolly for the AB Dick 360. To assist the Secret Service in their forensic investigation, I painted the entire floor this marvelous shade of green. Evel Knievel taught me one thing in life—if you're going to be a damn fool, do it with style, and people will pay just to watch you fail.

I pulled my Cougar XR7 through the drive-through dairy, pulling my crime scene along behind me.

"Leaving town so soon, stranger in the black hat?" the dark-haired damsel said as she stood about three feet from my car door, her feet at parade rest, her fingers crammed into the front pockets of her snug jeans.

"No, just drop-shipping some big orders that usually come in about this same time every year. The back-to-school season is almost as good as Christmas. I'm going to drop this stuff off, then go back to Santa Barbara and finish up business, and bury some assets along with some memories."

"Then you'll be stay'n on around here! Somebody's spread you got your eye on?" Then her tone changed. "You been spread'n just about everything in two towns I've heard!"

"Accusing me, miss, I can't be just one man's women," I said as I pulled out slowly on to the main street. "Commitment is a three-syllable word meaning more than one."

"Go to hell!" she yelled out after me. "Call me when you get back," she said as she turned to walk back into the store. She hated losing anything, including a verbal battle.

Who in town really knew me? How many had a clue that I was not what I pretended to be? The manager at JR's, Beaumont and Banning's only country western disco, where I rolled over a hundred one-dollar bills at a time. He thought I was a speed dealer. Most of the outlaws in town knew I had some game going on. The only thing they knew for sure was I wasn't gaming them, and I damn sure wasn't look'n for any new partners.

When all the while I was shooting darkroom proofs of over two thousand serial numbers. It worked out like this. One thousand eight hundred numbers on twenties, fifties, and hundreds, divided by twelve mint codes, divided by fifty thousand sheets of paper, giving you one hundred fifty thousand bills that were equal in numbers but different in their sum totals. For those of you who shrink from math, this is simple. You got fifty thousand twenties; that's one million dollars. Then you got fifty thousand hundreds, that's five million. Now if there were fifty thousand fifties, that would have been two and a half million dollars. If you add two more cases of paper to cover the edges you have an even ten million dollars plus waste and even is better.

*If they got printed, where is the used set of plates?*

After I went over to Hemet and off loaded everything, including the original unfinished ten million in hundreds, which were printed on four hundred and eighty-five dollars worth of paper that was cut wrong into pony sheets eleven by seventeen inches. I put six cases of counterfeit into the trunk of my car, dropped the trailer off where I rented it. Then I dropped off four cases of hundreds and fifties in a storage unit I had rented in Beaumont.

I needed to see Big Mac and touch base with Eddie. I remember I did not like Zuba when I first met him. He was half old family Mafia and a full case of nuts. I just figured I did not need Eddie the Grip listed in my jacket of known associates and I, the first time counterfeiter, did not need to be listed in his jacket.

Look at me, I'm an average Joe! Sure I grew up back east in the hometowns of the rum-runners and Mafia from the forties to the sixties. I would not have changed one moment of those times in Plymouth, Carver, and Middleborough. Those were the perfect days, and those heartbeats in prison were the not-so-perfect days. However, there I was doing lunch with people like Christopher Boyce, the Falcon, Eddie Zuba AKA Eddie the Grip, and Horace K. McKenna AKA Big Mac.

He told me once that I was the only one who ever called him Horace and lived, other than his mother. There was the doc, the one they named that wine after the year he was released from prison. The list gets even more impressive as well as their connection to brands of products and services that you see advertised every day on TV, along with all of those people whose names can still get you killed.

It was at Lompoc where I met the man who would become the "Iran Contra Gun Connection." They called it a gun deal. That's like calling the great train robbery a stick-up. It was an arms deal. There are nations in the western block that had less armaments than what changed hands in that gun deal. I never suspected that part of my destiny would become a part of this country's shameful, secret past and a lie that would create two wars!

Remove a single pebble from a beach and in ten thousand years, you will have changed the world. Life changes faster than that with a lie for which there is no truth.

Tuesday, Bogart was to check into the Palm Springs Hilton. I picked the place, but Bogart thought he was hanging there waiting for me to tell him where the drop is going to be. He did not know I would call him from the hotel payphone. When I hung up, I told the bartender to send a small bottle of champagne to Mr. Brent Pope's suite. That worked—the hostess asked me to pay the check, and Bogart's room number was on the ticket.

Bogart was so paranoid that he would rent two rooms in a hotel and leave instructions with the desk how to route his calls and visitors. So I knew the desk clerk would send the champagne to the room he was really in, and of course the bigger the tip the less questions you are asked.

"Do you need this?" I said to the hostess as I slipped the bill into the pocket of my three-piece suit and traded it for a fifty-dollar tip.

"No, that will be fine, sir. I do not need it." She smiled.

I had asked Bogart if he was ready to wrap this thing up. "Just tell me where and when," was his reply.

As soon as I had the room number I went to my car and removed the cases of counterfeit, premixed with twenties and hundreds, one million in each case. I grabbed my portable hand truck out and wheeled them in the side door and down the hall to Bogart's room. Before I knocked, I could hear Bogart and Ed getting all worked up over the champagne. "Who knows we are here?" Ed asked.

"Who knows we are here under the name Brent Pope?" concerned Bogart even more.

I wanted them rattled and not thinking, and it had worked. Who said paranoia is not a good thing?

I knocked on the door and the room went dead silent, except for a couple of *shushses*! Then came Bogart, trying to sound like someone he wasn't. "Who's there?" Why, I'll never understand that one.

"It's me, Bill," I said back like I was expected. He'll never understand that one. My sixth sense told me Bogart put his gun away. Out of sight would also be out of reach. I don't think Bogart missed the fact that they nicknamed me the Hulk in prison. I don't think he wanted to do any hand-to-hand combat with me. One more advantage I had was that people think if you've got big arms you're like a woman with big tits—no brains! Like it would just be unfair for the fit to be intelligent!

Bogart does not open a door when he is paranoid. He jerked it open like that's going to give him the element of surprise. He was so guilty; he was so unready to blow me away. That's the other reason I didn't wear my piece. It was going to go down my way and Bogart wanted more money than just the two million, of which he probably only leveraged one million. He also need-ed to know when the print shop was cleaned up so he would know I did not leave him holding a smoking gun, my insurance just in case Bogart killed me too soon. That would make me the winner in Bogart's book of reasoning. So Bogart was just standing there in half of his three-piece suit with his French ruffled shirt sleeves rolled up, his gold chains around his neck hanging out-side his undershirt.

*This guy seems familiar to me; Brent Pope in the book* Flight of the Falcon *is also Bob Martin and Lynn Dale Bogart.*

Yeah, now you know who I'm talking about. There was one other name that I used to call him by. This was the who and the what, along with the how. If pigs could fly, what does that mean anyway?

*That means you're Larry Harold Smith, AKA Big Larry!*

No, that makes me the one in the book who was the counterfeiter. I never robbed banks. I have no idea where Lindsey got that information from or that name. Must have come from the tiny mind of the K-Mart blue light special, Larry Hommenick of the U.S.-less marshals.

I stuck Bogart with the two cases of money so fast he did not have a chance to think. "There's a note and map in that case," I said, pointing to the bottom case. "It tells you all about where and when I will give you your split. You bring me my cut for all of this. I'll call you when it's all buried! When I call you, all I'm going to say is, 'time to pay the note'." Then like a good deliveryman I was out of there at a sprint.

Bogart would be trapped by his paranoia long enough for me to get all the way to LA. The drapes in his room were pulled closed tighter than a vir-gin's knees! My headlights hit his windows when I backed around to go out the entrance. That way if you got a tail, they're going to need to wag it, if they're going to follow.

I did not like what I saw. Federal heat—not to panic! Me and Bogart both had aided Boyce in his escape from Lompoc Max. Chris is still on the run and the guy who had a gun smuggled into MCC, San Diego, to make it look like Chris was going to break out from there by force was just visited by the guy who helped him acquire all the stuff he needed to break out of Lompoc Max.

If they were going to pull me over, they would use a black and white! The good news is I'm on the back road out of Palm Springs and no black and white in sight. I got no smoke, no coke, no guns, and no counterfeit money. Now let's see if we can make it no feds! This road is the best escape route out of Palm Springs, and the reason is you can just up and vanish. A dip in the road, lights out, a quick right, a quick left, and a quick car and its bye-bye feds. It's one way to the freeway and no way off until you get to the dinosaurs! By the time they get turned around and come back I'll be getting off at the first Banning ramp and take any one of three different ways into LA. Then on to Santa Barbara to see Teri and then up to see my kids, maybe for the last time in forever.

Nobody ever really reads the fine print. That's only if you lose anyway. Anytime you got what looks like easy money, you'll draw what bullshit attracts on the prairie.

With no way to contact me, Bogart wouldn't be able to change anything. He is on my string now. He will dance when I pull it. He had no choice—he had to pay off the debt first. The person who owned my pink slip was a coke dealer out of San Diego named Skip. If Bogart killed the counterfeiter whether he paid Skip or not, Skip would kill Bogart.

**You do not kill a working counterfeiter. It's rule number one of the outlaw code of conduct.**

No matter how you slice it, Bogart was going to pay but Bogart always had a rat hole to get down. Everyone is chasing their own destiny in this game. It really wasn't going to change things no matter what the "heat" was for. Someone had to die if someone's going to live to get away. If you're not ready to make these kinds of deals under these kinds of circumstances, do not acquire great wealth, power, political prominence, or become involved in crime, organized or otherwise. I've never met so many of the aforementioned until I entered life through that alternate door. I had only considered that if I failed I would go to prison. I had never considered that I would have to kill just to finish the game. I picked counterfeiting because it seemed like the only crime that did not require shooting someone.

*"Easy life, right this way, look out for the pit falls!"*

I stopped in LA just about the time the clubs were closing, so I took a chance I'd run into everybody at the place they called the "Penthouse." It was the entire top deck of a good-size apartment building owned by Big Mac, right in the hub of the LA basin. Pick a direction and you got a freeway. I took the private elevator to the only floor it serviced. You have to enter a steel cage with a key or be buzzed in! The only time I use my key is when no one is there to let me into the elevator. Cameras do not let anyone on the elevator or up the back stairs without being fully scanned. Everyone who was allowed in the Penthouse knew that sneaking someone or something into the Penthouse was dealt with by Tramp, the resident manager. Tramp answered to no one but Big Mac. The only question I ever heard Big Mac ask was, "How you doin', Tramp?" They went back to a time before, in the day.

*With things this bleak, you are going to party with friends? What were you thinking?*

Hollywood calls it schmoozing, business calls it networking, we call it showing respect! That's all we have on this side of the law to do business with. It allows the real players to keep money and merchandise in different places at the same time. Feds do not like just half a bust.

Most of us had a better up-bringing than the so-called officers of the law who come to get us. So it is necessary for us to have a place where only the right kind of people can get in. You know; the crème-de-la-crème!

I would rather be here with these people, locking the world out than to be anywhere else with those who did their crime behind the shield and the black robes of justice, those who have no loyalties on either side of the law, the ones that defile organized crime and the law.

What people do not seem to be able to comprehend is, you cannot get ride of organized crime until you do away with leadership government and the number one culprit, organized law enforcement with all of its sub-sidiaries. What, nobody ever drew you a picture of the vicious circle?

# CHAPTER FOUR

*You eat what* you bit off or you choke on it! Did I just make that up or is that another one of those old sayings? Remember: Mom said, "Finish what's on your plate!" How about: You don't get your just desserts until after you finish all of your shit sandwich! This is the second time I've been scared, because I just realized the reason I got scared the first time.

Your stomach rolls over for a reason. It's because your brain is sick of your stupid mistakes. It did not matter what the federal agents are watch'n for. You don't have to be dirty to get busted. They already know I'm doing something with somebody. That was a given when I started this and is the reason Bogart was against my involvement with Teri from the start. That's the reason I put space between Teri in Santa Barbara and my business in Palm Springs and my children at the other end of the state. My children will probably never understand why I just disappeared. Anything that any of them knew was of no value to the feds or to anyone else who might be closing in on me.

It was not that long ago that the feds tried to delay my release from federal prison until I told them where Chris was. It all started about three days after Chris went over the wire right under the guard tower window of the rear sally-port gate. There was a lot of tension in the camp because of the selection of the inmates that were being questioned. Glad I was not the first and fearing I would be the last to be called, I literally shuddered when my name was hollered out from the doorway of the captain's office. "Step in for a minute," a United States marshal said with a crook of his finger.

I was shocked when I was informed that I did not have to answer their questions, that I could in fact walk out anytime I wanted to. Oh man, I wanted to know what they knew. I was just days from a release date from Judge Thompson. So I said I would be happy to tell them what ever I could. That was not a lie! I know because the truth was what I could not tell them.

*"What were you thinking about when you were helping the Falcon escape from a maximum security prison? When you were only doing the short end of a four-year sentence in a nice kick-back prison camp?"*

"Isn't it true, Jennings, that you did time with Christopher Boyce at MCC San Diego, and isn't it also true that you, Bogart, and Boyce were what—tight?"

I did not like the foundation he was attempting to build. It was having nothing to do with what they knew and everything about what they could prove. So I flew into the faces of fools with my fifty-one-fifty act!

"You motherfuckers lock me up with a motherfucker, and now you want to make it a crime! Fuck you I'm out of here!" I hollered as I exited the room into full hallways, as it was count time.

Destiny does not require volunteers. Shit, contrary to public opinion, does not just happen. Hell, I had no idea. You see, I'd not walked this road before. You get to be thirty-something and you think you have done it all. Christopher Boyce was a little younger than me, he looked like my brother Jimmy, and he was a very focused person. He was my friend and we never defined what that meant. He was doing forever, and I was going home soon. When I look back at it, you have to choose. Was it a government scheme that brought these players back to the table over and over again? If so, I've been an anti-government agent since 1957 and did not know it, or bingo—destiny! We all know you do not choose destiny or we would all be born with inexhaustible trust funds. You know, like a politician.

We were both in the joint because of a personal beef with our government. We both came from unbroken homes of patriotic parents. We both came face to face with a truth that was so big nobody would believe it. I do not believe for a minute that any of that played a part in why I helped Chris with his escape. If the truth be known, I did not think he stood a snowball's chance in hell of making it out past count and I was not going to be the one who rained on his parade.

I never questioned that I was going inside a maximum security prison two days a week operating what was considered heavy equipment. Even though I knew, the rules prohibited it. I never questioned the drops I would pick up on the dump road or under the bridge just south of the camp farm road. I never troubled myself about how or who was paying and sponsoring Chris's escape on the outside. It was not real, as I carried out these tasks as it added a certain aspect of danger and intrigue that I am still addicted to today.

Reality did not hit me until one evening I was on my way back to the dorm and the sirens went off. I was terrified all night, waiting to find out who went over the wall. It was not until the next morning. I was making my way back to the landscape office to get my daily job assignment when a member of the Hawaiian Mafia and another currency major told me quickly, just when no one else was in earshot, saying "Chris went out last night and made it to first base before the alarm went off."

I guess that was when I finally realized that I had just stepped in it again. Technically, they could keep me until they caught him. However I had no idea at the time who had engineered his escape and was picking up the tab on the outside.

They were not going to let me off this easy! The next day Bogart was pulled in, then after the workday was over, after count, they called me in again. They were calling me in when everyone in camp could witness how long I would spend with the feds. Everyone else was interviewed during the workday.

This time it was a different room they pulled me into. It was the wired room, with mirrors and hidden cameras.

"Okay, Jennings, you do not have to talk to us, and you do not have to go home in just a few weeks if the judge rules in favor of your modification. I'm sure that Judge Thompson is going to consider your co-operation in the capture of the most wanted spy since World War II!"

"Jennings," another agent said over by the widow with a large heating-cooling unit under it, which dated the building to the fifties. "Come over here for a minute," he said as he pulled pictures from his inside pocket and laid them out on the large surface with impeccable lighting. "Look at this picture here. Where is that picture taken, Jennings?"

I was more interested with where it was taken from as he laid down picture after picture that had been taken over a period of months.

"What was it that you were drawing on the ground here, Jennings?" the agent demanded, pecking at the picture with his finger.

It was piss down the leg time, and I would have, if it were not for the big question—WHY? Why did they not only watch and let it happen? They made a photo log of every contact between Boyce and me. They even had pictures of every drop I made. I was beginning to feel like the man who just might disappear without a trace. God knows my family would believe whatever they told them! Even though it was quite evident, I was nothing more than a utility person. They would never dare walk into a courtroom and face a jury with the fact that some part of the federal government, working with an organized crime family and this farm boy/counterfeiter from Carver, Massachusetts, broke Christopher Boyce out of a maximum security federal prison! They do not have me, I got them and they have pictures to prove it! I have absolutely no recollection of what I said next. I found myself much later as I sat on the place we called hippie hill. It was a tranquil place to reflect and smoke the herb of reflection.

I had just received a letter from Judge Thompson that stated frankly that he was calling me down to his court on the second of June and hopefully I would be released the same day. I needed to be sure that the judge was not going to play ball with that slimy, zit-faced, Mexican U.S. marshal with bad teeth. He had told me that the judge agreed to not modify my sentence to time served unless I gave them what they needed! Translation: We ain't got shit, we don't know shit, and we can't prove shit.

Danny "O" was a high roller; you might say he put the "O" in organized crime! He had a manned phone deviator in Colorado. I would call the number in Colorado, the person in Colorado would then dial the clerk of the court for Judge Thompson in San Diego. He would put the whole thing in play for me.

Danny "O" was holding the phone for me at exactly eleven-thirty on the tenth of May 1980.

I was terrified, I was breaking a lot of rules, and I was doing it at a time when you do not want to be pissing a judge off. The phone rang twice and was answered with a mouth full of bologna sandwich. "Hello!"

"Hello," I returned and stammered, "is this the clerk of the court for Judge Thompson?"

"This is Judge Thompson. How may I help you?"

"Judge Thompson, I'm William Brian Jennings, you sentenced me on—"

"I know who you are, Mr. Jennings. I believe I sent you a letter? This is very irregular. We should not be having this phone call, and I'm not going to ask you how you pulled it off from prison! You are not a careless person, Mr. Jennings, so I assume it is a matter of great importance, so why don't you tell me why you risked this call?"

"Yes, sir, I mean Your Honor! The U.S. marshals told me if I did not tell them everything I knew about the Boyce escape, you would not modify my sentence. The marshals said you agreed to that, and you told them to tell me!"

"I'm going to say this very quickly, Mr. Jennings, then I'm going to hang up and forget this phone call ever happened. First of all, Mr. Jennings, the U.S. marshals have not spoken to me about you or the Boyce case. Secondly, I do not run my court that way. I'm calling you down to my court on the second of June and you will be released the same day. I recommend that you do not talk to the U.S. marshal until after I release you, and then let your consciences be your guide. I am looking forward to seeing you, Mr. Jennings. Goodbye and good luck."

I walked out of the phone booth like I was walking on two feet of air. Danny was nowhere around so I went out to hippie hill in search of someone to share in my euphoria.

After lunch, I walked over to motor pool, which is located outside the rear of the maximum security prison. I had done this two or more times nearly every day for the past seventeen months. This was the first time I felt the eyes of the gun towers watching every step I took.

When I entered the shop area looking for the camp's own race car builder, I spotted Dick putting his finishing rag on what had to be the world's best dirt track racing tractor. T-1 was a four cylinder Toro gang mower tractor until Dick modified it into a high-speed highly maneuverable smuggle-buggy with a spider front-end, duel rear wheels, and gearbox slicker than a grease spot on a concrete floor.

"She's ready to go, Bill," Dick smiled as big as a billboard. Dick was not only my mechanic, he taught me the fundamentals of jailhouse lawyering that won me a modification from a judge who had not modified a sentence he had handed down in over fifteen years. Dick had admired a soap sculpture that I had made, so it was an honor for me to give it to him.

Caressing T-1 like she was a fast woman instead of an ugly tractor, "Can she do wheel standing donuts now, Dick?" I asked, climbing into the only lawnmower with a seat belt at that time.

"Now don't go off and kill yourself. Remember, this is a prison! You are still getting modified, aren't you?" he asked looking concerned.

"Sure am, right after I drive T-1 up that repulsive bastard's asshole." I popped the clutch and pulled a modest wheel stand out the shop door.

I swear that at that moment I had no plan, I was just doin' prison chatter as I headed back over to the camp. As I approached the T intersection in front of the camp receiving entrance, my favorite U.S.-less marshal parked his car right at the far side of the T leg I was coming down. He locked the door as I changed gears and went to the floor with my right foot. The marshal turned and saw Donald Duck in Road Rage, coming right at him, going way too fast to make the corner. I turned the wheel to the left, then to the right, slammed the brake pedals through the firewall, and came to a dead stop.

T-1 was standing parallel and facing the same way as the fed car with only inches between them. All I had to do was lean over my right knee and put my face right in his and say, "Fuck you." Then I looked down and saw that my outside rear tire was going to go right over the marshal's cheap tasseled loafers. So I popped the clutch and spun the marshal right back around.

He jumped in his car and left. Ernie pulled me over with the boss's pickup truck and asked me if I had lost my mind.

I was laughing hysterically and gasped, "Do you think?" I left T-1 under a spreading pine tree and Ernie and I went off to meditate over at the camp dump in the boss's truck.

*This is prison; you drive around in government vehicles and smoke pot all day? No wonder they do not need a fence to keep you in. Then they have a guard to keep your old lady out and let your girlfriend in. Why did you want to get out of there early anyway?*

Freedom is not just a word, explained away with three misinterpreted phrases written by our forgotten ancestors. Freedom is getting up in the morning and going as far in any direction you want for as long as you want then changing course whenever you are moved to do so. Prison is a place where your heart cannot feel love even when you are holding it in your arms.

*But you seem to be having such a party every day, without a care in the world.*

We get our delight by proving to the government that we are the ones they cannot defeat as we hold the key to what they are willing to sell their loyalty for. The government has been fighting crime since before they crucified Christ. For two thousand years, the government has been promising to stomp out crime and lock up all those stupid criminals. Plus they get you to pay them huge sums of money to fail year after year. In the equation of government, taxpayer, and outlaw, tell me again who you think has the whole thing figured out wrong.

*Why can't they get the job done?*

They can't get the job done because they do not believe in the concept of honesty, and if they stomp out crime, who will pay them to be stupid and incompetent?

*I get it now, it's that vicious circle thing. Without crime one-fifth of the working population would have to compete for real jobs.*

**It's a rush, at least as good as cocaine!**

I get it whenever danger gets close enough to smell it in the air. Like the day I borrowed the printing press off the aircraft carrier, the USS *Ranger* CVA 61. So I could make a little adjustment in my income to make up for my low pay grade they jilted me into when I re-upped after an eleven-year gap.

It was pure inspiration! Never did I have doubts about our success. You know they make such an issue over rap music and how it puts bad ideas in the heads of impressionable children.

"Hogan's Heroes" taught me how to deal with prison. However it was "Mission Impossible" and "It Takes a Thief" that gave me the insight on how I would forge the documents that allowed me to borrow a printing press, paper, plates, and negatives from the navy. I got the captain to okay and pay for the use of a pick-up truck from base motor pool. From the officers to the crane operator, everyone was so helpful. I was so high by the time we got everything into the Holiday Motel, I thought I was either going to have another heart attack or ejaculate. Anything that feels that good in itself is addictive. Everything we experience in life affects our life. What we do with these impressions determines how we live it, good, bad, or indifferent. No one but you can determine how you live it. Life is an adventure and an experiment. Always changing, always new, and even in prison, life is what you make of it.

You know it your whole life, but when you're a kid you're just pretending. It's not my fault my older brother always made me pretend to be the outlaw so he could chase me down and catch me. How much do we know about our future when we are just kids growing up? Everyone in society is not going to learn the same lesson. Or is it better to understand that although we all go to the same well, we all draw different water. Can I claim that or did someone else already say that, too?

It's often easy to criticize others and the way they act or re-act! No matter how you look at someone else's action, remember it is not you. You really do not know what choices you will make until you have those choices placed in front of you for real. So unless you know how to print counterfeit and you have just been asked to print millions of dollars in counterfeit, for you to say I made the wrong choices doesn't carry an endorsement of value.

I was just really bugged at the Penthouse. I needed to get out of there. I called Teri, it must have been about five in the morning. She was preparing to leave for work. She told me she'd leave a key where I could find it and that she would be home around five.

That's when Tramp pulled my gun out of my belt and shot this mouthy pimp from West Lake. It was a lite-load, dum-dum, and the pimp was dressed in a real silk three-piece suit. So after everyone's ears cleared, Mr. Express from the lake of the west was asked to leave before Tramp finds out what's in chamber number two! Tramp shoved my gun back at me like he had been cheated, quite literally, out of death.

"I've got a three-fifty-seven that would have turned that boy into chip beef. You want it Trash?" Tramp said quite abruptly. Trash is the nickname for counterfeiters and people who hang bad paper. However, I have been nicknamed Trash since my last Vietnam tour aboard the USS *O'Brien* DD 725.

"I know," I replied. "That's why I load light. I believe in second chances!"

"I like you, my friend, but you're wrong there. No one gets second chances, 'cause no one paid for the first chance. That's why life got no refunds—when it stops, it's over."

Tramp grew up in Torrance, California, so I have no idea where that came from. No one ever said, "Here's an old California saying."

I stopped by one of my roadside storage units and picked up four well-wrapped bundles of counterfeit totaling one million dollars, plus four other smaller bundles. The government provides really great hiding places that do not require hiking shoes or shovels. Them and John Deere tractors, God bless 'em!

Arriving hours before Teri, the guy on the utility pole above me was assurance I was not alone. Seventy percent chance they are just watch'n with a thirty percent chance they were ready to pounce! I did the in and out shuffle, then I made a run to the corner market and back again. Between that and trimming the bush out front and taking out the trash, I managed to stash a million dollars under the heavy Chevy on blocks just outside Teri's living room window. It was real difficult getting it under the low side. That would also make spotting it from the driveway impossible. The removal will be done on the downhill side of the car, even if that means when I come back I will have to walk up from the Earl Warrens Show Grounds.

When Teri arrived home, I was just a bit edgy! Teri was either going to dump on me or she expected that I'd only returned to leave again and never come back.

Never and forever, two more lies in the English language. No wonder the Indians say "White man speaks with fork'ed tongue." White man got too many fork'ed words! We didn't really fight, and we didn't really make love. Without words, we both found our own way to say goodbye while we cut our own deal with our hearts.

When something is good, you should not have to wreck it, just to say goodbye. How easy that looks on the outside. From the inside, it's impossible to imagine. Killing love when it's young and fresh seems as desolate as the death of a child.

That's how it feels on the inside. Love is a life of it's own. That next morning Teri opened her telephone bill. She was sitting in the kitchen with her back to me. I turned around from the sink counter with my coffee in hand. Teri was puzzling over the irregularities of her photocopied phone bill. I was not surprised; even so, I snatched the telephone bill from behind.

"What's wrong?" she asked, surprised and thinking I was overreacting.

I did not have the time to convince her of what was happening. The guy on the pole, the photocopy telephone bill. Somebody was making a case, and I was it! I told Teri to leave the house as normal as she could. "Go anywhere, just go," I said with enough emotion for her to grab her boys, her handbag and hit the door. I then made a dummy phone call. I let it ring three times and hung up. Then I grabbed my jacket and started for the Cougar. I stuck my hand out in front of me as if to check the time. Then I turned ninety degrees to the right as if the sun was a problem. I continued the ten or so more steps to my car, as if I had the whole day and nothing to do except shit.

If the feds are ready to pop me, the best thing for me to do is act like I'm just about to do something or meet someone. The second thing I want to do is become that stupid con they think they're watch'n! Right now, they would let me pop a priest if they thought I would lead them to Christopher Boyce.

They were going to let me run my rope all the way to the end. It was my job to unhook it before they jerked back on it. Kind of like what we did to the Middleborough police car back when I was a teenager. We had chained the rear axle of the police car to the phone booth down at the Rotary Circle. Then everybody raced right by the cop car. The difference this time is I'm the one about to get jerked back.

I did the back and forth thing to the car, stopping out in plain view, just stretching my back, and openly smoking a joint. Then finally I had their signal lock in on my Concord scanner.

*"Look at that stupid ass out there in front of God and"...."I can almost smell it from over here"...."I can smell it over here, I'm down wind, pure gold"...."Yeah, well if you were making the kind of money he does you could afford the gold too, ha ha ha"...."Let's just see if he leads us to Chris"...."To hell with Chris, just lead me to the money"...."The money is not our problem"...."Nobody gets to Jennings before he gets to Chris"...."Then everybody can have him!"*

I was ready to move! Okay boys let's go to Paradise and visit my children. That way when I made my break the feds will drop a blanket over my kids and nobody is going to risk that just for get-even money. There were still a lot of pitfalls ahead that made for a lot of bridges to build.

Everywhere my kids and I went that weekend, three fed cars went with us, the same three from Santa Barbara. Who you are by the car you are tailed by. Okay, any fifth grader can spot the FBI and the DEA in any shopping center parking lot. The CIA and the United States marshals don't get any harder unless it is a K-Mart parking lot.

Now there is a pair to draw to. Botany 500 and the K-Mart blue light special. Ever hear the one about the wife of a U.S. marshal? She said to the K-Mart manager, "How much is that suit on the dummy," as the blue light went round and around? "I got a dummy of my own at home just that size."

When I went to the office of the Ponderosa Motel in the Pines, as I'm a regular guest, I would pay in cash for the weekend on Sunday before leaving.

"No, no, Mr. Jennings, your money's no good here today." The very healthy good-looking couple who owned the resort said with a smirk. "Show him, dear," Dave said to Sharon, his wife. "Show him the receipts."

Sharon fanned out ten room receipts. "And they all checked in within an hour of your arrival time," Sharon said with a smile.

"Then they had their wives join them Saturday! Some of them have already made reservations for next season. The best part is federal credit cards always clear with no returns," Dave added not missing a beat.

"Whatever you're doing, Mr. Jennings, we hope you get away with it. You have such well-behaved children and we enjoy having them and you stay with us. Good luck, and may God bless you."

We had three cars left over from the losers-only demolition derby and this black car I couldn't even identify the manufacturer. If I did not know better, I'd say it was Mafia, all the way from the homeland. As far as I knew, they did not have a beef with me. They were not my problem. They looked more like they were tailing the "Key Stoner Cops," i.e., the U.S.-less marshals.

Everyone lined up in front of the garage door and we kissed goodbye. Tracy, my oldest child, knew as she stood in the road and waved a solemn goodbye until I was all the way out of sight that Daddy wasn't coming back.

I had managed to plant two five thousand dollar bundles of money for my children, should I have a need for them to have it. They would know the spot where I waited for them in the woods behind their house. That money would lead them to where the one million will be buried if I made it back to Santa Barbara without a convoy.

# CHAPTER FIVE

***You always know*** what you need to know, even when you do not understand the feeling. It starts way down small in your stomach. Was it lunch, or is it intuition? Am I going to throw up or get busted? By the time I know for sure, my head is either stuck in a toilet or I'm stuck in the back seat of a fed car with my hands in cuffs. Either way it's my day.

Bogart must have been desperate. He called Big Mac and left a message for me. He tried to reach me at the Ponderosa, however he was told I was not registered. As I had not paid yet, they were not telling a lie.

*How does one manage to be ready for all of these variables in your daily plans? Do you remember what you were good at as a kid and how in some way it is connected to what you do in life?*

I was the shortest kid on the court, but you could not stop my running, jumping, half-court hook shot! Even so, I did not grow up to be a basketball star.

The other thing that I excelled at was something I taught myself while playing good guys and bad guys in a place we called "Cowboy Land." The back of my neighbor's farm had a grove of young pine trees. They had taken over an unused pasture. They weren't much bigger then we were at the time. It was a perfect place to play.

My brother and his friend Jay would chase me into this place called the box canyon. When they would come up on me from behind, I would drop down on one knee, turn, and shoot up into them at close range. We used cap guns with live caps in them, real dangerous stuff. I got to practice it over and over again, because I was always the bad guy!

When I arrived back in LA, Zuba needed a driver and bodyguard for a transaction with some people he knew very well. They had a reputation for being less than reputable. The closer you get to the brick wall, the faster we seem to go. This is the part in the movie that the music gets louder with a lot more base.

"Are we expecting them to try and stiff you, Eddie?" I asked, not even giving a damn. Why should I worry I'm with Eddie the Grip?

35

Anyone who ever drove to LAX knows that it just is not fun, but try it in a limo. As I turned down hotel row, searching out the massive structures for the entrance to the Airport Hilton, I pulled in and parked on the left side of the main entrance. All of the white curb was occupied with limos, cabs, and rental cars.

Eddie and I both exited the limo at the same time. I clicked the trunk open as I stepped out. Eddie reached in and retrieved the standard stereotype coke dealer's briefcase. I pressed the lid closed and checked the ride of my jacket over my gun. Eddie looked like Zorba the Greek, with his shirt open halfway down, his massive chest adorned with gold chains and silver hair. Somehow the people just knew instinctively to move aside as we pressed our way into the lobby. We went straight to the elevators. I paid no mind to the button Eddie pushed. I was numb by the feeling that prison was closing in on me and I did not like the feeling at all. I covered Eddie's back as he led the way down the hall to the suite.

Eddie rapped on the door, and it was opened by Big John. Yes, I called him Big Bad John. Not only did I know him on the streets, but I knew him from prison. Blond hair pulled back into a long ponytail. His receding hair-line, massive build, and piercing blue eyes made him a good partner to hit the clubs with. I watched him pat Eddie down. It was his job and it was part of the ritual and the facade of the people who were prepared to kill anyone who did not play by the rules. John opened the door and Eddie proceeded into the main room. I hesitated, waiting for John to pat me down. He just slapped me on the back and gave me the go-ahead nod. I stepped into the next room and John closed the door while remaining in the entry room.

I was standing directly behind Zuba, to my right were two goombas I did not know. They were standing at the window with one of those stylish wooden chairs with the plush crushed blue-gray velvet cushions between them, their hands folded in front of them. They did not appear to be packing. Rick was standing on the far side of the bed with a full-length mirror to his back. Rick used to drive for Big Mac and we both liked western-cut three-piece suits. I could not help noticing that Rick had on a really well-cut jacket.

Zuba stepped forward and opened his briefcase with forty-five pounds of uncut cocaine on the bed. Then Rick opened theirs with the money. That's when I noticed in the mirror that there seemed to be something under Rick's briefcase. Suddenly an argument started when Rick said something about testing and weighting it. I eased my left foot over just enough to allow myself the ability to see around Eddie. I slipped my right hand slowly up my back under my jacket, pressing the safety off while pulling my snub out and firing two short loads into Rick's gut right before he could level, point, or fire the .45 he had pulled from under his briefcase. Rick slammed up hard against the mirror. Eddie reached out and grabbed the gun from Rick's limp hand as he bounced forward off the mirrored wall. I dropped to one knee as I spun around just as John opened the door with his .357 magnum ready to fire. He froze when he felt my snub nose pressed up against his balls. Meanwhile Zuba pumped two shots into the pretty French chair, turning it into kindling wood. Eddie pushed the revolver into his pants, grabbed both briefcases, and we made our exit before they could think what to do next.

Eddie was pissed. "Weight it, test it—who do these punks think they are doing business with? Five years I knew these assholes. They been buying from me since I started back up here."

"You think Rick is okay?" I slipped in between, Eddie's cussing.

"Sure he is, you just shot him in the gut. We own doctors all over this town." While we were in the elevator Eddie handed me both briefcases and took both guns.

We exited the elevator and stormed through the lobby and out on to the drive. Eddie hit the trunk button on his key ring. As I dumped the two briefcases into the trunk, Eddie used his handkerchief to wipe off Rick's gun and throw it in the shrubs in front of only about one hundred eyewitnesses. He tossed me a look and a gesture over the roof of the limo. We jumped in at the same time, Eddie in the back and me behind the wheel. I quickly got us out of there and down to the Ramada. I pulled down into the subterranean parking. While I put on the other set of plates, Eddie registered us into separate rooms. The desk clerk handed me the a key to my room. "Are you okay sir? You look a bit flush," he said as he handed me my key.

# CHAPTER SIX

*Your whole life* you wonder if and when it comes right down to it, do you
have what it takes to do what it takes. There are a lot of wannabes who pack
iron but could not pull and fire it instinctively, even if it was at someone they
hated. Rick was someone I knew quite well, and shooting someone you know
because he pulled iron in a gentleman's deal was not something I learned at
Governor John Carver School. I didn't learn it on the street growing up in
the ghetto. I learned it growing up on the farm, watching Gene Autry
movies, "Leave It to Beaver," "Father Knows Best," and "It Takes a Thief."
Yeah, it would be fair to say I was confused! I guess you have to do time to
understand the code of ethics that has to exist at this level of play. Eddie Zuba
was from the old school. He won his reputation back when the Tommy Gun
was the loudest voice in town. He did the things they made the movies about.
This green as grass farm boy was the one he picked to watch his back. I was
duty bound to shoot Rick and now my head is stuck in the toilet, wrenching
my guts out.

Eddie knocked on the door, then let himself in with his own key. I was
lying down on the bed by the time he got all the way in the room. Eddie
knew me well and said very little. He ordered everything that I was going to
need. He turned on my TV and made three more phone calls. Then he came
over and sat down on the other side of the bed. "Do you know how Rick is
doing?" I said, just barely able to speak. I knew Rick was not likely to die
from the two dum-dums. It was like being punched very hard with a tiny
fist, twice. He would be down for a few days and walk funny for a few more.
Rick was not buff and had a bit of a beer gut. I think the reason I was heav-
ing my gut back then was that I could not believe how easy it was for me to
act out that scenario as if I was an animated figure in a computer game.
From the very first time a live revolver was placed in my hand, I've been able
to hit anything I pointed it at. It was the same with a rifle, from the waist I
can walk a beer can down the road. In the navy, I was labeled from boot
camp as marksman.

I think it goes deeper than that. DNA = Destiny Not Accident! We hung there at the hotel for the next seventy-two hours while a truce, an agreement, was negotiated. Rick's people would pay up front 75 percent of the next four deals and get credited 25 percent of the money Eddie already had. The deliveryman will have a loaded gun in his hand for the entire transaction. If they are pack'en then they would be shot and they lose the holding money. Rick's people sniveled some until they were told that first delivery was that day, and it was going to be Trash holding the gun and that I wanted Rick there so I could see he was okay. No, I was not unusual. I, too, had come to believe that honor among thieves was dead. However here and there you could still find bastions of integrity.

I had not intended to stall Bogart this long. Even after I did this other little earn for Eddie, I needed at least forty-eight more hours to get everything set for my meet with Bogart. I needed to do it on a day that the dump was closed. The only place that one could see the backside of the hill was from the gatehouse on the dump road. Even though the view was partially obstructed from that side, no chance is a good chance to take.

Bogart was leaving messages with Big Mac and Zuba's service. It was a private service made to sound like just another business. However the girls knew how to take down a message and forward it the way it was meant to be done. So when I called under the name "the Ayatollah," they knew who to give the message to. Big Mac gave me that telephone handle in the joint; he thought it was funny. Bogart was begging for a meeting. Translated that meant "or your kid falls off her bike on her way home from school."

Feeling a little different about my plans for Bogart, are we? Well as shit would happen, it did. While I was off picking up a total of just under a half million dollars in cash the old-fashioned way, Eddie and just about everybody else I knew picked a fight with a half-dozen federal narcotics guys. Actually, Eddie started the whole thing because he was tired of doing the same thing day in and day out. He said it was getting to be too much like doing time. "So, I kicked a little federal butt," Eddie was saying as I walked into his hospital room over in San Pedro.

We did the "how you feeling" stuff. Eddie had shoved his fist down the throat of this federal agent and got a gash on his hand between his thumb and forefinger. It had swollen up as big as softball. Now you know where the term dirty rotten feds came from. The nurses were dropping by and doing lines off his bed table. Of course, Eddie made them kiss him first. For Eddie everything had to be as big and as loud as he was. You don't find people like him in the library unless he is there to kill the librarian.

He could see I needed to talk in private. He waved everyone away. I told him I was going to meet Bogart. "He needs to talk to me," I told him in confidence, close to his ear.

"You got your piece with you?" he asked, holding me by my shirt so I had to look him dead in the eyes when I answered him.

"Yes," I replied.

"Put it here under my pillow," he said. "Or better yet, don't go. Pack your shit and lay dead. He probably set you up for a bust."

"Got to go—ain't no way around this. We got heat, true, but as long as Boyce is free their best chance is Bogart or me."

It was a gamble either way. Running and hiding wasn't in me. I put my gun under his pillow as I stood up and leaned over him, giving Eddie the Godfather kiss on the cheek so all of the nurses could see. I have to admit that I got some pleasure from preserving the elegance of the past. Everything I was doing seemed so natural. I took a double blast of coke and waved good-bye to everyone.

From there to the MacAurther Airport Hotel was about an hour. I tried to put my thoughts to rest on the way out. I slipped across the backside of Long Beach, jumped on the 405, and headed south. There were hundreds of things I would have wanted to be doing other than what I had to do today. I knew Bogart was not going to hit me now. That would not serve any purpose from which he could profit. He could be setting me up for a bust, or he could need to see me for the reason he was claiming. He claimed to have enough to pay me off. He wanted to push up the payment of the note. He claimed to have fifty thousand dollars he wanted to give me up front.

All my sensors were telling me that shit was about to happen. If it was a bust, I was clean. Clean except for what went up my nose back at the hospital. I forgot that 90 percent of the money in my wallet was counterfeit. I pulled through the parking area and saw nothing that looked placed except for a dirty old green Pontiac. I pulled back out on the highway and went up far enough to pull a tail if I had one and I didn't. I pulled a U-turn and headed back to the hotel. This time, only one section of the parking lot was opened and they were setting up for valet parking only for the noon hour. I parked in the section with the ugly old green Pontiac.

When I was a kid back in Carver and off where I should not be, doing things I knew I should not do, with Ikie, Barry, or just my dog Rusty, I could always know whether I was going to get a whipping or not when I got home. Trust me, it was always well earned. Right in the corner where the back porch hooked up with the main part of the house, near my sister's bedroom window, there was a big glob of black roofing tar that had oozed down that inside corner. Sometimes it looked like a happy smile, and other times it looked very angry. I hate to tell you how many times I was right. It was not coincidental that old green Pontiac gave the look of the angry old tar on the side of the house and it sent a chill down my spine.

I parked my Cougar facing the hotel, just to the left off the entry port. As I walked to the front entry, I handed my keys off to the valet. I thought I would order food if Bogart was not already here. I was the type of person who preferred to be early for my appointments. There are all kinds of habits that we have, and habits, even good ones, can get you busted.

The hostess took me right to a booth, so fast I barely noticed the chore-ographed layout of the people seated around the restaurant. Before all of this happened I had fears I might be just a bit paranoid. The hostess tried to seat me on the wrong side of the table. It was awkward for a moment as the tan-gled web began to twist and bend. Oh yeah, this was going to turn out bad. I was set, but not busted. If they had enough they would not put on a show like this.

Bogart seemed to have come from inside the restaurant, out of the cor-ner of my eye, it appeared to me. My instincts were raging by the time Bogart sat down. Was he wired? That question answered itself. Just as soon as his little rat tail began to wag, it began to grow.

"What about the other ten million dollars?" was Bogart's first question.

What was wrong with that, besides the fact that he had known the other ten million was not worth the time and paper it was printed on. I had not liked it from the day he delivered the paper that was cut completely wrong. Yeah Bogart was wired, so let me take this opportunity to point out to the feds that as it was uncompleted, it did not constitute counterfeit money. If that was all they had then it was nothing. So after I made my point I made for an exit! My gait was large as I walked out the front, across the drive. As I passed, the valet tossed me my keys. I did not wish to look behind me for fear that it would impede my departure. Once in the car I looked down to place the key. When I lifted my head, four gun barrels were pointing at me from each corner of my Cougar. Then those famous words rang out like a pierc-ing dentist's drill.

"Jennings, you're under arrest. This is the United States Secret Service." Another agent grabbed the door handle of my car. He pulled the door open and me out faster than anything I could think to do to stop it. Without stop-ping the agent pulled me from the car as he ran his hand up my back like he was trying to retrieve my gun from my pants. All the time the first agent con-tinued to say, "You are under arrest," as I was being rolled down the side of my car and flung down on to the ground. When I looked up the first thing I saw was a rifle with a camera mounted on it pointing at me from the roof of the carport. It seemed like they had set me up for a kill. If I'd been pack'en they would have had the motive to shoot me dead right there in front of hun-dreds of eyewitnesses. Meanwhile another agent pointed his gun at the peo-ple who were walking into the restaurant and hollered, "Freeze!" As two agents threw me over the trunk of my car, I witnessed one pleasingly plump lady wearing a faded black leotard as she sprung a leak that spilled down her legs and on to the sidewalk. If I had been her, I would have sued! Unfortunately, I was the counterfeiter in handcuffs. Thankfully, the cocaine was still with me and at the right stage to help me get through the next seventy-two hours of the rest of my life. Little tiny cracks in my armor appeared as I was on the fast track back to federal prison. I must make bail, so at least I will have a choice when I scratch for my last card in the game. Whoever said that our jails and prisons were just merry-go-rounds never took the ride.

I had no misgivings when I went into this. If you think it was not smart of me to try it in the first place, I could show you whole pages of statistics that could demonstrate it to be otherwise. Anyone who has ever gone into business for themselves knows that even in honest business you can wind up face down and in cuffs.

They have not convicted me yet, nor am I in prison yet. Right now, I'm going to be booked. That's sort of like riding the "L" train at rush hour in Chicago with your hands in your back pockets.

That was all very encouraging until I found out that Bogart had been busted three days earlier and they had let him run around until he could corral me in Costa Masa. I guess the Secret Service cared more about making the largest counterfeit bust ever in the State of California and the second largest ever in the United States more than they cared about me or Bogart leading the U.S. marshals, the FBI, the CIA, and the KGB to Christopher Boyce.

"Money is the root of all evil." I'm sorry that is incorrect! Greed is the root of evil; money is the food that greed eats. I was only producing generic greed food. Somehow I was thinking that Joe would know how to talk his way around this. When times get heavy, you must think relaxed or get taken over by your emotions. You can be as emotional as you want after they turn the key and turn out the light. They want you to be all anxious and edgy. Just pretend that the longer it takes to put you in lock-up the less they have to keep you there. So enjoy this time with the feds, and remember things could be worse. You could be one of them, born with hormone-displacement syndrome.

It took longer to clear the arrest scene than it took me to print the money. They had found enough information in my car and my wallet to pinpoint one of my storage units. Unfortunately, it was the one with everything but the good money. So I co-operated and gave consent to search.

I knew what they had. Bogart could only speculate based on what I let him know and most of that was not true. The feds were going to be very confused if they could even figure out what I'd done—the unused case of paper that seemed to be totally different from the product that I produced, the remaining fifty-six printing plates, which had no value once they were used for reasons of identification.

I was put in the back seat of the old ugly green Pontiac for the long ride into LA. I had gone around in a circle but I had not ended up where I had started. Then they kept me in a little cubicle until well past midnight. They would drop by and tell me how much information Bogart was giving them. They also wanted me to know how good a deal they were going to cut him for all his help. My reply was, "Then you don't need anything from me." So about 1:30 A.M. they hauled me out the back door of the Federal Building and through the back parking lot. Everything was wet and there was a mist in the air. We were moving fast with a fed on either side and me with my hands cuffed in front of me.

Some idiot called out from behind us, "Mr. Jennings, wait!" He called out more than once until I hollered back that he should make that request to the two idiots that had me in tow!

Finally, the madness was halted. It was another fed out of San Diego. He got permission to talk with me for awhile in private. He started out by acting how impressed he was to have a chance to talk to me in person. My only question was why could they not have gotten a female fed to kiss my ass. Obviously, Bogart had not given them anything but me and a whole lot of wild speculation. Federal agents have very limited imaginations, thus they believed everything Bogart told them and nothing I said would change it. However the stuff I was denying to know anything about was the stuff that I knew never happened. I figured if Bogart could get these idiots to believe his bullshit, then just think how much better my bullshit would fly once I played the hand they dealt me—this Secret Service Agent who claimed to know about my prior bust and how impressed he was with the whole "Mission Impossible" printing press thing and how they all still talk about it down at the secret agent watering trough.

However after that he got closer than I allow most women and inquired as to Zuba and Big Mac's involvement in the counterfeit operation! It was really lucky he had not fallen for my ploy to take the cuffs off so I would be more comfortable. I backed him into the corner of the steel cage they put us in and read him up one side and down the other. "If that's what Bogart gave you, he gave you shit you can't make stick!" I was so angry that the feds did not understand me after all they knew about me.

I raised rats when I was about ten and sold them to universities, so I know what happens to rats when they get put in little cages. I'm almost locked up and absolutely not one agent asked me about Boyce yet.

The Falcon had flown the coop more than eight months ago and they still did not have a single clue. It was the weekend so they got to hold me for the max before arraigning me. It was Sunday evening when I was called out for a visit. I was expecting that there would be a chance I'd get a visit. My friends would send in a stripper to find out what I needed. What I got was three suits in the "common visiting room." No, they didn't stick out too much in a room full of bandanas and tattoos and Chicarone girls dressed to instill a speedy return to the streets.

I was introduced to Larry Homminick, who acted like he was giving his best impression of a bad-ass federal agent of the U.S. marshals. That will get you a big scoff from the FBI, who declared marshals are not agents, they are just marshals. Now are you beginning to see the flaw in having so many whores working the same corner? Pimps do not do it, but the feds do.

"All right, Jennings, they got you cold on this counterfeit case. We might be able to help you out a little."

"Great," I replied. "Do you think you can get this case dropped, give me about two hundred and fifty thousand, and a brand new Canadian identification?"

"Well, no," Homminick confessed, "but you don't understand. If you give us the information we know you have regarding Boyce, your life will be in great danger. Everybody wants him dead. He screwed the Russians. He sold them worthless bullshit for millions."

It was a large room with tables and benches, accented with stainless steel and the ugliest color of floor tile ever put in a public dining area. It was not very crowded. No one was really within earshot. It wasn't like everybody wanted to have their visit next to some feds. I did know what he was implying, however I played the dumb inmate I'm supposed to be. Make him spell it out for me, give it to me by the numbers. You were only smart if you took their deal and dumb if you didn't. They seemed to have no idea of such things as principles, integrity, or just plain old self-esteem. I guess what I hated about them the most was their low personal sense of credibility. These people put everything of themselves up front—money, safety, security, and their next promotion. It was all more important than the job they were getting paid to do. Every other word out of a federal agent's mouth was that it made him look good or it made him look bad. Here is a dollar, Jack, tell someone who cares. They thought that I shared their value system because I was an outlaw. By the time we stopped taking shots at each other, I told them to go climb a rope. "Go climb a rope" can be used in a court of law. What you were thinking is not palatable for a courtroom. Plus it speaks volumes should they try to use the tapes they were all wearing to block my bail.

As I walked out of the visiting room, Homminick hollered out, "Thanks for all the information you gave us about Boyce, Jennings. We will catch him for sure now thanks to your help, Jennings."

I panned the galley of inmate eyes and as my eyes met Larry's, every inmate in the room flipped Homminick off. Homminick did not understand that being locked up and being stupid was not always the same thing. If they are so smart, how come after more than two thousand years we still have prisons? They blame it on the Constitution; I blame it on them for not obeying the Constitution. Remember, criminals will always know how to get out of prison; honest law abiding people aren't that gifted. Believe me, the Constitution is your only hope!

They did not roll me up with the morning court chain, so I figured I was going on the afternoon chain. Then I was rolled up real quiet like, just about ten A.M. Two suits escorted me to this courtroom that was full of press. The judge pushed it through real fast for only fifteen thousand dollars. I begged the judge to please lower it, I was just a poor guy working all alone and did not have that much, which was only fifteen hundred dollars to bond out. The feds had to let me make a phone call to make bail.

There I was on about the third floor. The press got zip! I got chump change for bail. My two male escorts stood close enough to hear me say, "Tell both of them that my bail is fifteen!"

"Fifteen million?" the girl's voice cracked back at me.

"No!" I chuckled. "Fifteen thousand dollars!"

"A fifteen hundred dollar bond gets you out, Trash—I mean Mr. Ayatollah?"

I was so embarrassed—wanted dead or alive and a fifteen hundred dollar bond! Boy, I do not want to fall on this now; I would never live it down in prison.

So you can imagine how surprised I was to go past nine P.M. and not get released! The next day they did the same thing all over again. The only thing was they took me in front of another judge. My public defender was there and the prosecution table had new people sitting at it. The new judge had a big smile on his face. The courtroom was closed and empty. A man in a four thousand dollar suit reached out and touched me on the leg as I passed by. He made me aware that he had my bond covered and to ask for a bench release.

The prosecution claimed that they knew that I planned to escape and go to Canada. The judge quickly told them what value he took in the tape they submitted as evidence to raise and/or deny bail while holding nothing back as to how pissed he was that they did all of that without my attorney being present.

One million—no, ten million. I told my lawyer, "Hey, I only printed ten million." I just could not believe what I heard next.

The judge continued, "It seems to me that the amount of money that a counterfeiter prints when a counterfeiter prints money is only determined by the amount of paper he has, and Mr. Jennings just happened to have a lot of paper." Bang went the little hammer! He set the bail at a fifty thousand dollar cash surety bond.

In lay terms, that is, "Give me a briefcase full of money and Jennings walks." My public defender never knew he was such a great attorney. So I had to yell out as the Judge was reaching for the doorknob to his office, "Judge, make that a bench release!"

The judge walked close enough to the bench and grabbed his little hammer and bang, "Make that a bench release," he proclaimed and left the room. As they took me out the bail bondsman was covering the deal.

# CHAPTER SEVEN

*I had over* four hundred dollars of counterfeit money in my wallet when they busted me. They only seized one unfinished one hundred dollar bill that I had secreted in my wallet. How much did Bogart give up, or did he just give me up? Checking out of Hotel LA was a bit difficult. I had to go out front to get my boots, belt, and my valuables.

I could not believe my eyes as they counted me out four hundred dollars in twenties from their cash draw. Thank you, LA County Jail, for no charge laundry of four hundred dollars of counterfeit. As I turned around to face the street, the big courthouse steps were to my left, and I spotted a fed. I quickly spotted the bondsman, looking like a five-year-old doing the potty dance. Before I could ask him what he was doing there, he gave me the keys to a Lincoln Town Car and an envelope containing several large. "No thanks, friend," I said as I gave him back the Lincoln key with the rabbit's foot key chain. "You take it back, give me all of your pocket change." He had a handful, I grabbed it all and bolted for the city bus. The driver was black and he just looked at me standing there with a handful of change and my clothes that looked like they had been in a box. He knew that the game was afoot. The bus driver's name was Watson, I noticed, just before jumping off at the first stop. I ran across the street just in time to bag another bus. I finished getting my clothes on right on what looked like the "crosstown cleaning lady special." They were having a good time at my expense, only in Spanish! I know enough to know when I'm the brunt of some humor. Maybe with a little luck I could get a proposal.

When I got off that bus I was too close to even get a cab, and I did not need to be hanging out on a street corner. So I walked down a few back alleys and cut across a parking lot and a used car lot to the Penthouse, where a shower, some great food, a soft bed, and someone who smelled good to sleep with awaited me.

Bobbie hollered down at me that she would beam me up because my key was cut as soon as I got popped. There was a bunch of people I did not know

47

at the Penthouse. It seemed Eddie was claiming he paid my bail, that Big Mac, was too cheap after they upped the ante to fifty large in cash! Big Mac, in his non-assuming way of the six-foot, seven-inch, 315-pound professional weight lifter and bodybuilder, merely grinned and said, "That's what Eddie said, huh."

There was not a single picture of me in any of the papers that ran the story. When Cronkite ran the headline coast to coast, he did not mention my name, only the deed and that I'd done it before. I was not in a safe place here. I was beginning to feel a lot like bait. I just did not know whom besides Boyce that I was tradable for. I had no idea how much leash they were going to give me. My bond was bounced out of Chicago because it's against the law for one ex-con to pay bail on another ex-con, and a whole lot of other reasons that are better for our side. Now you know why our legislators made that rule—because it made it better for organized crime and they were paid well to do it. Same reason they want the public to think that it is against the law for ex-cons to vote. Yeah, just as soon as they are ready to give us our tax-exempt cards along with our prison release card!

Just imagine—if you let ex-cons vote, why you could end up with a crook in the White House. Why they may just figure out a way to steal an election. Kind of like giving the country the finger. In America, our Founding Fathers had the good common sense to make the servant government responsible to the people or we just withhold our tax. If you cannot vote, then you also cannot pay tax—that's the law. So why is it that children pay tax when they work?

If you are committing crime with big dollar signs then you must own a Republican or know somebody who does. There are very few Democrats who have ever carried any real power over the courts that enforce these new laws. The Republicans have gone way out of their way to let everyone know just who owns the biggest share of the U.S. Supreme Court.

You must understand that these laws only protect the crime family territories. The police serve and protect the neighborhood organization. The prosecutor prosecutes and makes his best deal with the defendant and the judge can always be bought or replaced.

The candidate with the biggest crime bill is pocket bound to the biggest organized crime family in their district. It was no mistake that I made bail. It was in everyone's best interest.

However when it came to my life, the numbers were not in yet. I was still a major player and connected to a whole lot of people I had not even met yet, but you can bet the feds knew the names.

There was this saying in federal prison: "If you got ten friends, eight of them belong to the man." On the street, if you know ten cops, organized crime owns eight of them and the other two are on the waiting list. There should be a great sadness in your heart to know that beneath the lost loyalties of honor among thieves lies the best of the best that you call police! If there is a lesson in all of this, it is, Make sure that you are registered with the right party when you get arrested, and do not get busted just before an election of change.

*Were you a major player because your counterfeit was so good, or because of the people who you were affiliated with?*

Even though I did not know it at that time, it was a whole lot more than even that. I was a major player because of my product and the people who were my friends and colleagues. The biggest point was right now I was not in prison. Whether or not I go to prison would be determined by how much time I will get. Right now, I needed the feds to proceed unobstructed and then beat the conviction through the holes they leave behind after they sentence me. The citizen does not have any loopholes until after they tie the knot. They had to convict me because that was the way they said the evidence proved it went down. Or they made the penalty small enough to make it not worth your while to fight it.

You thought that these things were perhaps just spontaneous, spur of the moment, uncalculated. Maybe for the common criminal, stick-up men, bank robbers, and the lot. The feds do not label your crime sophisticated unless the level of calculations is as high as a crime can score. There is no such thing as a perfect plan, criminal or not, or it would not say right in the scriptures: Shit happens (that is loose King James!). At this level you eat the shit sandwich or leave your prior life behind. Freedom or family is the choice I have until the hammer falls. I needed Boyce to continue to be free, long enough for me to do one last Christmas with my kids.

The next day I contacted Big Mac, I wanted to get out, move around. Big Mac called me back and said that he was picking up his new limo and if I went down to the street in about fifteen to twenty minutes, he would be curbside.

I waited about five minutes and went down to the street level and within two minutes a limo pulled up and a very large well-dressed man stepped out and I jumped in and quickly found myself in a limo without Big Mac. The limo pulled down the street just far enough to pull into a Safeway shopping center. The driver's window came down and the man on the front passenger side turned to address me as I was dead in the center between two very large men. He opened his shield and displayed his diplomatic card and his KGB identification card.

"Mr. Jennings," he said like he was from right next door, "we do not have a problem with you. In fact, we admire your resolve, or you really do not know the whereabouts of Christopher Boyce! We want to make sure that you understand one thing very well—whether you know anything about Christopher Boyce or not, you *do not* know anything about Christopher Boyce. Do you understand, Mr. Jennings?"

"Yes, sir," was my reply to the KGB!

The car pulled out the back, down two blocks, and dropped me off right out in front of the Penthouse, but not before the man in the front seat reached out the window, shook my hand, and wished me luck with my future.

Seconds later another brand new limo pulled up and the back door popped open. "Hey, Ayatollah," Big Mac called out to me. "Jump in. Where you been? We've been driving around the block for ten minutes."

I explained the whole thing to Big Mac and he didn't say anything. "Don't you understand that the KGB has got your phone tapped? How else they gonna know when to pull up in a brand new right off the show room floor limo?"

None of this seemed to make any difference to Big Mac until I mentioned that I thought that the KGB had a better-looking model. Now we have violated Big Mac's Constitutional right to have better limo than the KGB.

"Them bastards are bankrupt and they got a better limo than me!" Big Mac swung his head down and looked at me as he started to laugh. With his bigger than life chuckle he set the limo to rocking or we just hit some big dips!

The next day the limo went back and Mac got a limo that was not going to be outdone for a long time. That's what started the limo wars in LA back at about the end of 1980! Everybody started doing colors. Midnight Frost, Wine on Silver, Champagne, and psychedelic red and gold.

I had called Teri, knowing she had to know I was out. I asked her how she felt about that and she said she did not know so I said goodbye. Time would confirm that she did get it back then.

Eddie made sure I got stuck with the keys to his limo in my pocket that afternoon. "Hey, Billy," he said. "Look, my old lady has one of her friends down from the Bay Area and she needs an escort because we are going to hit some clubs then go to the Penthouse. You know, a night on the town with our old ladies."

"Look, Eddie, I'm out on bail. Don't hook me up with some over-the-hill mob widow."

"Hey, you do not have to do anything you don't want to but you do have to bring me my limo. I'll get you a cab back to the Penthouse if you still want to after you meet her."

"Okay, Eddie, I'll be there in about an hour. If I'm going to be up for twenty-four hours, I better shower first."

When I got to Eddie's, I had to go around to the back to get in. His house hung out on the edge of a cliff on the ocean side of San Pedro, with a more splendid name and a better view. Eventually Eddie came out of the master suite to thank me for coming over and bringing him his limo. "Hey how would you like to earn a couple grand and drive me and the ladies around tonight?" He shoved two grand in my shirt pocket and stuck my gun in my leather jacket.

"Diane, that's my old lady's friend," Eddie said, obviously quite hammered. "She wants to pick out her own man so we just need a driver." Then he turned and went back down the hall. Before I could walk back over to the couch, Eddie was back at the arch entry to the hallway. This time he had his arm around the neck of this totally hot, tiny woman! She was not but five feet tall! Her hair was a shade of honey gold used only by God for angels, hot angels. She was in every way every woman I had ever imagined during my whole life. Eddie did the name thing back and forth. Then Diane said to Eddie, "Tell him that I want to sit on his face," and she did not appear to be drunk or high.

I held up my hand to check the time. Diane laughed and said, "I tell him I want to sit on his face and he checks the time."

I replied very calmly, "You're wanting to sit on my face and I just want to make sure I have sufficient time to give you the ride you desire." The next thing I knew we were sitting on the couch so close with her hands in mine and I was telling her about my children, the whole time cussing God for pulling this terrible trick on me. I am facing up to fifteen years and now he sent me the one I'd prayed for since I was old enough to know you could pray for girls and not go blind. It was not just her beauty; it was her restless spirit that would jump up and down with my spirit every time we would come together in the same room. When it came time to get in the limo, Diane said, "I'll ride up front with the driver."

I did the door thing, seating Diane first. How do you think God punishes us sinners anyway? He was just out there rocking back and forth laughing out loud. I sometimes think that is what keeps me alive—God likes the entertainment my life provides for him.

Come on now—you are given a chance to watch my life or yours; which would you choose? We left the house just about eleven-thirty and arrived at Mac's new Hollywood Club about one o'clock. Diane wanted to know how many of those girls I had done. Of course, I did not look at the girls or Diane when I answered her question.

I did not want to fall in love with her and I was sure she did not want to fall in love with me. It was like trying to pull apart new Velcro for the first time. We both did our best to get involved with other people the whole night. It did not work—we just ended up right next to each other like our clothes were stitched together and I could not stop looking at her. If this was

God's punishment for me counterfeiting again, then I'm going to take it like a man. A broken heart is better then an empty heart. The next day it was decided that we would all drive up to Diane's home in the East Bay to put a sound system in Eddie's limo.

Of course Eddie tried to beat Diane down on the price, then I casually interjected that perhaps he could not afford the best system, then maybe he should settle on something cheaper. Diane shot me a look like was I stupid or something.

Zuba reached his hand into another pocket and quickly added the disputed thousand on the table. When Diane picked up the money she pressed up against me and shoved a hundred dollar bill in my pocket while giving me a quick kiss.

One of Diane's sidelines was installing sound systems in limos for people other than movie stars and motion picture studios. You do not just happen to be best friends with Eddie the Grip's lifetime wife and not have your own worth.

We had not slept yet, so Diane kept the coke ready should I get the nods, and she read me stuff about two sages in a relationship. I do not recommend that anyone duplicate this experiment without a lot of emotional insurance. You are going to need a lot of it. That first visit at Diane's was one of the most profound times in my life. Nothing was right and yet everything was perfect. Her daughter Kim won my heart when she came down the living room stairs when we came through the front door for the first time, with her face just beaming. She was just about thirteen, with her brown hair, dark eyes, and freckles, she could not have been any cuter unless she had fallen from heaven straight into my arms. Her son Dean was too good looking for his own good, and the littlest one was Sonya, about the size of a bug and twice as cute. They instantly fixed the cracks in my breaking heart while putting one more reason for "not running" on that side of the equation.

I was out on bail and restricted to the greater LA area. The fact that I was in San Francisco was not known to the feds yet. The feds did not even know I was living at the Penthouse yet, just the KGB knew. They did not know I was driving Eddie around. Believe me, we know when they are there and when they are not. Diane kind of made me a little challenge. If I really felt all this love for her, she said, "Why don't you tell your probation officer that you want to live up here with me until you go to prison?"

Then she walked out of the bathroom in her bathrobe and bare feet, stood right in my face, and slapped me. "Bastard!"

Yeah, like court probation was gonna just care so much about my feelings. However, Diane was not the kind of woman you just shined on about anything. If she said it she meant it, and I had so much trouble understanding it because she was so profound I could not believe it. She was like my mirror self in every freakin' way!

*That sounds like any guy's favorite woman, the mirror of themselves emulated in perfect form. Oh yeah, I'm there!*

Yes and when we fought, we fought with fangs and talons. That only served to heighten sexual tensions that never seemed to end and sex was the end of every fight we had.

*You are using the word fight, but you do mean argument, don't you?*

You be the judge. We would start out arguing about something we both agreed on. After about two or three hours of tension that had the kids heading for high ground, then I'd get right in her face and call her a bitch and she would slap me so hard that my ears would ring for about the next twenty minutes. She would leave her hand in the air so I could grab her by her wrist and force her down on to the bed. It was like a cycle, and each time I would ask her why she would make me go through all of that when what we both wanted was this. Then she would laugh and throw herself on me and say, "Want some more of THIS, Mr. Jennings!"

*Yes, well, I think that answered my question.*

You cannot duplicate those kinds of emotions, nor can they be recaptured. Once they go away, they are gone forever. All the romantics in the world know that solemn truth to be told. Nothing dies like love. It was also the final perdition in the book *Sun Signs*, the one prediction we would fight for many years to come.

You cannot spend all of the time that you're out on bail worrying about going to prison. Diane understood that really well and she was one hell of a diversion. I had a lot of anger and frustration.

*You were mad at the feds for busting your counterfeit operation?*

No, contrary to public belief, I hate the feds because they represent everything that is wrong in America and why so many of us are made to feel that this is the only means by which we can achieve a quality or value worthy of our effort, abilities, and talents.

I was mad at myself for blowing it again. However I was not as hard on myself this time as I was the first time. I remember one gloomy Sunday morning at Camp Lompoc. I was just sitting there in the chow hall when old Doc sat down and said, "You look to be down on yourself."

I had not been there very long, however I knew who Doc was. I felt honored that with plenty of seats available, he chose to take Sunday brunch with me.

"Well, Doc," I said, "I was just thinking what a total fuck-up I am. Can't even break the law and pull it off."

"Whoa, now, hold up just a bit. You are a counterfeiter, right, William, or do you use your middle name Brian with an 'i' not a 'y'?"

I was taken aback by the stuff he just happened to know about me the first time we talked.

"Put things in perspective," he continued. "If you played baseball and you only hit the ball every other time you come to bat, you will be an all star. If you played basketball and scored every other time you shot you would be a super star. However, when you are an outlaw, all you have to do is make one mistake and you are busted. Do you think I'm a fuck-up because I'm here?"

"Why no, Doc, but you're worth millions!"

"That's right, Mr. Jennings. You are in here as a member of the Millionaire's Club. If you never succeed past this point, you will have experienced more success than 55 percent of the people will ever get to experience in their entire life and you have the extra gift—children, children who will bless you with grandchildren. Tell me, Mr. Jennings, you set out to do exactly what?"

"I set out to print two hundred and fifty thousand dollars."

"And?"

"And I printed two hundred and fifty thousand dollars!"

"And you got busted because your passers got busted because they did not follow your instructions?"

"Yes, Doc, that's how it went down."

"Unlucky without doubt, but a fuck-up you are not," Doc replied.

Just then the camp administrator came into the dining room and stood intolerably close to our table and Doc whispered as I stood to make my departure.

"This is the definitions and an embodiment of the term you referred to earlier," he added in a low voice.

"Good morning, Camp Administrator Cage," Doc said as he decided he didn't need the indignity of the proximity. Cage was our own Colonel Clink, whose wife must have been a big K-Mart shopper. I saw him in stuff no self-respecting mannequin would be caught dead in. Most of the time it didn't even fit. They look more like her boyfriend's size, left behind in the bedroom when he would have to leave in a hurry. Then she would say, "I just got that for you at K-Mart. Try it on dummy!"

Cage had a sweet teenage daughter; I spent a very nice few hours with her one afternoon. On a bus from Santa Barbara to Lompoc, we shared a couple of joints. First, we smoked one of hers, and then one of mine.

*"Didn't she know you were one of her Daddy's inmates!"*

Stay with me here, it's the late seventies, you're a teenage girl and your daddy is a prison warden. You go to school with the children of the inmates and you're not brain dead. Of course, she knew who I was as soon as she saw me on the bus. In fact, she asked if she could sit with me and took the window seat so she could roll one for us.

I walked into my probation officer's office. "What can I do for you, Mr. Jennings?"

"I want to change my residence to this address on this form I already filled out here."

"Your connection to this person is what?"

"She is my wife, in the eyes of God, not in the eyes of the law. Do we have a problem with that?"

It wasn't like her name was squeaky-clean nor was she the pillar of the community. She had one of those secret jackets that is better than no jacket. Every time the feds write themselves around the Constitution they open the door to the other side—crime. They keep trying to outcon the con. That is genetically impossible! The Constitution is the best anti-crime bill ever written, if the government obeyed its standards, crime would not be our problem—finding menial laborers would be our biggest problem.

None of what I proposed was any problem in the world. "When do you want to move?" he said with a smile.

I lifted my arm to check my watch. "I can make the two-thirty to San Jose," I returned as if I had already bought the ticket.

The probation officer stood, shook my hand, and wished me the best. I went straight to the restroom and washed it before I put it in my pocket. Then I went back to the Penthouse, grabbed my bag, and snagged Tramp to give me a ride to Zuba's office at the airport. Eddie was in a meeting with two old ex-Mafia friends who were selling futures for some new kind of TV talent show. I did not have time to wait. Besides it was legal and Eddie seldom invested in legitimate commerce unless it worked like a laundry machine. Eddie introduced me to Louie and Ed, then we all shook hands. Then I told Eddie I wanted the money he owed me for services rendered.

Eddie played this for all it was worth. Basically I was quitting and I wanted to collect all my marbles. The thing was, no one quit Eddie the Grip. He could fire you, let you go, or retire and live, but quit you did not do! Those gentlemen in the room knew the young Eddie the Grip would shoot you in the back when you turned to go if you quit him.

Eddie reached into his desk and brought out his bank deposit envelope and unzipped it. Then he laid down five thousand dollars. I held up three fingers and he paid me eight. I thanked him, grabbed up the cash, and headed for the door. Just as my hand gripped the doorknob I heard the distinct sound of a hammer being locked back and ready to go. "Gonna miss you, Billy, but you will be back, just as soon as she chews you up and spits you out. She's a man eater. Remember you got a home here with family."

"Oh shut up," I replied.

As soon as I had my ticket in my hand, I called Diane and told her I would be there in an hour and twenty minutes. I would be arriving San Jose on Western Airlines at 2:55 P.M.

"I'll be parked right out front in the White Zone," and she laughed. "What, you did not think I was going to run all over the airport looking for you? Or be waiting at the ramp with roses in my arms and tears in my eyes?" Then she laughed some more as we hung up the phone.

Of course I was happy, but no, I did not consider myself lucky. I was in the Bay Area because it was in the man's best interest. It just worked out that it was what I wanted as well. They thought I was just trying to connect up with the Falcon!

*It is almost like a greater power was orchestrating a stage for you to play out some playwright's vision; but how did this serve the purposes of the feds?*

When you get deep enough into life you begin to understand the real foundation of the old sayings. They take on a whole different meaning. "Enough rope to hang oneself" sounds like something I can relate to!

# CHAPTER EIGHT

*We landed on* time and I rushed toward the White Zone out in front of the terminal. First I heard Diane, then I saw her. Like the bouncing ball above the words in the song she jumped and bobbed around in the whirlpool of people. The kiss she gave me there in the busy airport terminal told me she was pleased I filled her request.

I found myself in the position of not having my own car. Diane had enough vehicles to have her own auto show. Two show trikes, a Harley Sporstar, a 1932 Ford on a Mustang frame and running gear, two show vans, a show car called Hotel California, and her gold Cadillac Bertz. It was obvious we needed another car!

I had not even moved out of my suitcase when Bogart told me he had been given the Cougar back from LA central impound and if I wanted it back he was more than willing to continue to float the lease.

Diane and I burst into laughter as soon as she hit the speaker phone button and ended the call. "We will make a fortune if we just sell off all the shit the feds loaded it up with," Diane attempted to say without breaking up.

"I think you should get Denis to upgrade my sound system so we can see everything we won," I added through snickering teeth.

"How you want to do this?" she said.

"Do what?" I replied.

"We got to go to Palm Springs and pick up our car."

"We!" I returned.

"Yes. We are going to fly, so do I buy the tickets on my credit card or do you buy them at the airport for cash?"

*You could do that way back then?*

"Let's see, Bogart called me on your phone, so how do we suppose he got the number? Get the tickets on your card and in our names. We don't want anyone to get lost or miss the trip."

Diane shot me with her finger. She got me with her first shot. We would take off tomorrow, leaving the household in the care of Denis, Diane's devoted domestic handyman and earn runner.

We did not need her Concord bug-busting equipment as we knew that half the passengers on that plane would be federal agents. We also knew that there would be enough electronics on and in the Cougar to fly it if it had wings.

We took off from San Jose, landed in Ontario, and changed planes for the hop into Palm Springs. The inconvenience was compensated by the sideshow being put on by the slick, stealth-like moves of our best federal agents. How often do you see people in mid-stride going in opposing directions exchange briefcases? If they were outlaws, no one would have ever seen it happen.

The flight into Palm Springs might as well have been a private charter as it was just us and the feds. My pistol was in Diane's make-up case in the false bottom of the upper tray. The good old days when it was still safe to fly, back when the terrorists knew the outlaws had guns and dying was not why we were flying, back when the cops had to check their guns and the people were safe, because in prison we have to learn how to survive without the law and the badge.

It would have been nice if Bogart had just dropped the car off at the airport but that was not the plan. Diane and I were just waiting to see how ridiculously they would attempt to involve us both in an indictable offense so they could use it to roll me over. It is kind of like waiting to sit down to a meal that your mother-in-law made just to prove she could not cook. You know you are not going to like it, but it comes with the marriage.

Bogart was late, as he needed to give the feds long enough to get set up to watch us receive the Cougar. Which, of course, had been scheduled to be picked up two days ago. Ed, Bogart's flunky, needed it for some lame story Bogart invented. Then, of course, he could not bring it back. We had to go to Hemet and pick it up at Ed's mom and dad's mobile home.

By the time he got done making up stories, Diane and I were booked into the Palm Springs Hilton on someone's credit card that came with room service, so I knew it was not Bogie's card.

The next day Bogart could not get free until almost eleven, so Diane and I entertained ourselves in the hotel gift shop. She bought boots, a handbag, and a jacket that looked like it had been made by a psycho trapper. While managing to keep the sales clerk in stitches, she dropped eighteen hundred dollars in less than an hour. It was a good thing I didn't meet her before Bogie or I would still be printing money today just to keep up.

"How many years have you two been married?" the sales clerk managed to choke out through desperate gasps for air.

Diane and I laughed as I said, "Her? I just picked her up in the parking lot out back!"

"No, go on—you two know each other so good and you enjoy each other like no other couple I have ever known."

Diane and I would puzzle over those same things along with our families and friends. We were like two eight-year-olds and the world was our sandbox. The nicest thing our friends could say was that we must have been Bonny and Clyde in our prior life. Thinking about that makes me sad. In the movie, I cried when they died together.

Bogart showed up late and took us to lunch on him like he had all the time in the world. When he realized that I was not going to have any discussion outside Diane's ability to witness, he decided to just spill it in front of her.

Seated in a sunny window booth of the retro '50s cafe, Bogart had the Mark Seven body recorder stuck in his inside jacket pocket. Nothing fancy and very tamperable, in case the feds needed to alter what was really said. His story went something like this: If I killed this waitress named Patricia McNulty for him, they would not have their probable cause witness and no pretense under which to have popped him and the whole thing would have to be dropped.

I could have killed Bogart right there on the spot. However I said, "Let me think on it for a few days, Bogie. Meanwhile, if you are done let's pick up the car so Diane and I can get started on our vacation."

He almost tried to allege that I should kill McNulty as payment for the Cougar. It was difficult but I finally got Diane's stiletto heel out of Bogart's crotch as she made him sit up straighter than he had in some time.

When we arrived in Hemet, Bogart grabbed the opportunity to let me know that he hid the microfiche in the retirement home of his partner parents. Boyce had traded the microfiche to Bogart for a phony attempt to smuggle a gun into MCC San Diego, which resulted in Boyce's transfer to Lompoc Max. Bogart and I both knew how much the microfiche would be worth on the open market.

*Who would buy microfiche that could easily be created, made up, or just plain faked?*

You do mean other than the movie studios who could themselves verify the authenticity?

Bogart had left his sport jacket and the Mark Seven in his Lincoln Town Car. I had to puzzle over that one, as I knew what those nine sheets of microfiche concerned themselves with. Chris had liberated them from the place known as the "Black Box," facts that the government still deny today that prove they know what they have denied since Roswell! I know it too; I read the titles of over nine hundred pages. That and a quarter gets me a cup of coffee.

So we were off and on the road with the Cougar, on holiday, no kids and no cops, just a few bugs that we treated like a perfect opportunity to do audio porn. The feds could entertain themselves in their blacked-out Ford vans.

Just before leaving the car Diane would ask me a question about my crime. I would lean over to Diane and say in a hushed voice, "I'm only going to say this once and you must never disclose it to anyone."

Then we would jack up the sound on a Joe Cocker tape. Then I might say, "I love you, babe," or something lewd or vulgar. We would take turns doing the sucker lines. Diane was also carrying heat of her own because of her long-time connection to a lot of hardball players. From Hollywood to San Francisco, rock'n'roll to rock'n' drugs, she knew the major players. So like another car, she needed some more heat.

This is the real reason we wanted the Cougar. It was fully wired, so we knew when we were in the Cougar we were on stage. This would pacify the feds and they would not let Diane get popped while I am in the house.

We spent our first night in a high-end Hollywood hotel. Diane told her kids that we would be home in about three or four days. She told Vincent, her life-long friend and hairstylist, that we were on our honeymoon. Then she told him to check in on Denis and make sure he is paying attention to the kids. "Make sure he is not spending all day in the jack room, backing off," she said just before hanging up.

The next night we spent in Santa Paula and visited another one of those special characters people like Diane and I attract. People who are truly different, not weirdoes and crackpots, as the rest of the world sees them. The way we see them, the true jewels in God's crown!

The Daisy Lady, as she was known, her and the yellow and brown bus, left behind in the wake of the hippies and flower children era. She gave us a reading of our spirits, "Your spirits are bound by a greater promise of love that comes from our spirit dwelling place. Stay not, for you are separate. Your fires will consume you! Your love will endure the test of time to bring you together whenever greater strength is needed by either one. These things you cannot and must not tamper with."

She did not need to explain the meaning of the many things she told us as we passed the pipe of friendship, love, and understanding. Then she married us in love and spirit before God.

All the next day Diane berated me about stopping in Santa Barbara. She insisted I go and say goodbye to Teri. Then she would harp on about me leaving her alone in a beachfront motel while I went off, and she would not stop.

She continued to badger me with it when we stopped on Santa Clause Lane. I made a prediction that once the real estate values reach a ridiculous height, the city government will decide that Santa Clause should be condemned as an issuer as it is not conducive to Santa Clause Lane. They made a movie about it. It was called "Dumb and Dumber: City Government and County Government."

Diane nudged me and said, "No fair!"

"What's not fair?"

"Not fair. You are supposed to be worrying that I'm jealous about you going to see Teri tonight and while you're gone I'm going to pick up another man and lock you out if you get back too late." Then she took a deep breath, heaved a sigh, batted her eyes at me, and I lost again.

We checked into the Seaside Motel and I went off to Teri's. Not for the reason Diane thought or the reason I should be there. I went to get the money and by now the feds would have their ears on. They would be torn between watching the motel and following me. They might have a lag problem. If I could get to Teri's after dark, in just two minutes those bags would be in my trunk. The driveway was on the corner of a hillside of a narrow street. You enter blindly until the front of the car dropped down so you can see the parking area. Teri's car was not there, so I swung my car around and backed in at an angle, covering the entire access area where the heavy Chevy was up on blocks. There were no lights on in her townhouse, so I popped the trunk lid and went around to the back of the car. I disappeared to the dark side of the Chevy, jerked out the black trash bags, stashed them into the trunk of my Cougar, and pressed the lid shut.

The silent trunk latch is the result of the industry listening to their most important car buyers. How many people got busted by the sound of a trunk lid being slammed shut? Here is a hint—Henry Ford, the government, and organized crime sharing one backscratcher. Seat belts had to become law before the industry would include them in the vehicle. Silent trunk lids showed up with not so much as a struggle.

I jumped in the car and began to scribble a note to Teri when a car used this driveway on a blind corner to turn around. So far the timing was perfect as I went to Teri's door and stuck the note in the jamb.

As I pulled my car to the top of the drive, Teri came bounding in with her little green Opal wagon. I backed down and parked in front of her. We went in. It was uncomfortable, but I was honest about why I was there—at least the part I could be honest about. I told her that Diane was waiting for me at the motel. Teri did better than I would have under the same circumstances as things could not get more impossible, I accused myself.

Teri did not come to the door; she remained on the couch that sat under the picture window with her back to the Chevy, looking down at her toes hanging onto the coffee table, her arms folded across her breasts. There were no lingering goodbyes to let them know I was on the roll again.

They would assume that I was going back to the motel, especially if I started out in that direction. They would also be ready to depart in that direction and the back-up unit would be parked on LaCumbra Road. So I would just make the rats run backward, by hanging a right and doing my back street magic. I came out on LaCumbra Road, over the hill, and the other side of State Street, from where the pit crew was waiting for me.

I raced up the highway toward Lake Cachuma, exactly five miles from the State Street light to a pre-designated spot. I turn my lights off, spun the car around in the dirt, pulled out, and raced down the hill far enough to encounter any tail I might be wagging. I turned my lights off again, spun the car around, and raced back to the hiding place. I quickly dispatched my task, burying one bundle on one side of the highway by the two big rocks. I know, it is so clicheque, so on the other side of the highway I buried the other bundle next to the ponderosa pine tree with a double axe scar, on the fifteenth of October 1980, at slightly past nine.

Again I was off and running down the hill with my lights off until I encountered the first intersection where I turned the lights on. Exiting on Cathedral Oaks, I cut across the back of Santa Barbara and then headed straight to the Seaside Motel.

The feds knew all of the big movers and shakers in the area. Santa Barbara was known for many things at that time—the home of the newly-weds and the nearly dead, and the best pot in the state was grown right there. It made it the perfect place for pot growers and the drug market traders to meet. You know, what they call a cartel today.

Some of those players still live in the local area. They now are either in the local government or they own the local government and most of the prime real estate. They created a large group of tax burners who are hooked up to the man who used to sell the drugs. Now he buys the votes with government paychecks that are guaranteed to rise regardless of ability, talent, skills, or economic justification.

They outright own over five thousand government payroll votes, plus the spouses and sheep that follow the twice-paid government job junkies. The rotting sewer system is an indication of how deep the corruption goes in this sleepy, beautiful, hillside bay community, a place where the homeless are still treated like criminals instead of victims of their crooked government.

It was ten o'clock when I arrived back at the motel. It was not too late as Diane had not finished freshening up. She had taken a bath and had that look in her eyes that told me I should take her. I knew I should take a shower first and rid myself of the dirt, the sweat, the guilt of the lies that had been told.

*What did Diane know at this point? Did she know what you had really done that night? Did she know you still had millions of dollars under your control? Did she know you still had deep feelings for Teri?*

That would have to come under the need to know, and you do not need to know. At this time I had no idea what was going to happen next. Outlaws have to learn how to plan for the unknown factor. There would be no long-term benefit in Diane knowing anything more than what she needed to know. What she figured out on her own she would keep to herself for the same reason. We were close enough and smart enough to know the difference between lying and covering. She did not tell me all about her business for the same reason. So we left Santa Barbara behind us for lunch at Pismo Beach and the night at the Madonna Inn on the coast. "The Caveman Room" was taken so we settled for the "Sky Blue Mountain Room." In two more days we were going to be back home and still together in a way I just did not understand.

It was the first part of October, there was more then a fair chance that I could remain out on bail until Christmas. After that, would depend on how much time I would be willing to do before it tipped the scales in favor of leaving the country.

*So you never intended to use Boyce, not even as a last ditch effort to get a smaller sentence.*

Don't make me throw you out of my truck! I want you to know that I would not be sneaking across the border and living in poverty the rest of my life to escape the perils of three hots and a cot. Like those guys in the old movies living in the tropics, hiding out from some dastardly deed, and wearing those damn white suits.

No, I would not be living like that, outside this country. Not with my trade, my reputation, and my connections! I had a little black book and inside that little black book were at least three telephone numbers. I could dial any one of them and there would be a limo at the curb and a private jet on the runway with clearance to go anywhere!

When the Secret Service rate the counterfeit bill, they have two scales: one to prosecute you with and the other to feed to the press. I rated up in the top one percent on both scales and they would make me pay severely for that. They called my bills a "ten." Therefore, they used words like "highly sophisticated." I had eighteen thousand different series numbers on only ten million dollars of twenties, fifties, and hundreds, so they claimed a threat to the economic security of the nation. Hell, most Congresspersons blow ten million their first week in office. It isn't like it was something for nothing; destiny has already proven that.

International law enforcement functions on high-quality counterfeit currency. It is the money deals are made with in other countries and used by undercover federal agents.

*Let me get this: The government busts the counterfeiter and then uses the counterfeit money to do business with other criminals. What sort of stuff would the government buy?*

They do more than that; they fund governments and terrorists we oppose publicly with counterfeit money, just to keep turmoil in the world, for when the tail needs to wag the dog again.

*"All of this will become more believable as we go on," he said and then drove the old pick-up truck right over the edge of the mountain. We were careening down the side of the mountain out of control, as terrified as the word can imply! "Then came Halloween," he continued.*

I had my kids at Diane's so I could take them trick-or-treating one more time. Then there was Thanksgiving and I had my children with me again at Diane's and we both cooked that year and surprised two sets of children. Diane knew what was important to me and the things I needed most, and no matter how hard I fought it off, she would always provide it, showing me over and over again that I did not need to be this immovable rock.

Women, who have no insight, say men have no emotions or we do not know how to express our feelings. It's usually some cold, insensitive, whiny, sniveling, why-me-mentality bitch that is babbling that crap.

Maybe she read me so well because our birthdays were consecutive to Thanksgiving and the end of November. Whatever was going on between Diane and I, it felt like heart-crushing love, the kind of love that hurts just the same as a broken heart.

It was about the fifth of December when things were getting a little tense. The longer we were together the less time we had left. Yeah, it is real easy to understand now, but impossible when you're the one careening down the hill out of control.

Diane was sitting on the bed in one of her many beautiful sexy night-gowns. Diane always looked like she was torn right from the pages of *Penthouse* or *Playboy* with or without make-up in t-shirts and jeans or dressed to the tens. With her box of bills and checkbook in her lap, she was looking at me over the top of her reading glasses.

"Sit down some place or get out of here," she fired out over the music that was coming from her state-of-the-art sound system. The phone rang and Diane methodically laid her task aside and reached for the elegant bedside phone.

It was for me, it was Eddie. All I said was "Yeah, gut-ja'ya!" I reached in close to Diane and hung up the phone as I gave her a kiss. Then I grabbed my keys, my rings, and my gun from the bottom of Diane's panty drawer.

As I grabbed the bedroom door, Diane said, "Have a good time, babe, and come back in a better mood or we're going to have a nail-scratching face-slapping fight." The smile on her face told me which way she wanted it.

I drove to Fry's parking lot, pulled up to my safe phone, and noticed a 1962 Chevy Impala, pinstriped and detailed, with two very large tattooed gentleman in the front seat.

I made the call and Eddie, said, "Right near your phone is a '62 Chevy Impala."

"Yeah," I replied.

"Get in it and go with them. They will tell you where they are going and what you have to do when you get there."

At this point, I did not care what it was about. It was quite possible that my friends felt me to be too much of a security risk and they were going to off me. The feds were still pushing for fifteen years and I had made no deal yet. So I climbed in the back and said, "What's up?"

"We got six suitcases full of money we need checked out," replied the huge neck in the passenger seat. We wound up out on the Monterey Peninsular at this very large white three-story motel. It was a rainy, drizzly night and a long, cramped ride to get there.

They were not kidding. When we got to the room on the third floor, there lined up on the floor were six huge suitcases. The blond-haired bone crusher who had driven me here went right to the phone and called someone in another room to go get food.

The other large-necked man threw one of the suitcases on to the bed and I started in, stack after stack, bundle after bundle. Time and time again, I would throw out a hundred dollar bill, then another. It must have been close to sunrise when I finished. I had thrown off two very large stacks of hundreds and one of twenties. I began to jog up two large stacks when the one I found out was Larry said, "No, Trash, you can't take that money. We got your envelope with two large in it here," he said, handing me the envelope from his back pocket.

"Oh, I do not want any of that stuff. It's counterfeit," I said as I took the envelope and thumbed the top of the bills.

"All of that is counterfeit?" the one named Frank said.

"Yes, just about one thousand hundreds and about a hundred and fifty twenties," I said as I scratched my neck and cramped another cold French fry in my mouth.

"Are you sure, Trash? I mean how do you know? You went through that shit so fast, how could you be so sure you got it all?"

"I know my counterfeit when I see it. Those hundreds are mine! The twenties are mine too. The only difference is the twenties are from my first counterfeit beef and the hundreds were not completed when the feds took them from me. They were still six to a sheet and no serial numbers on them."

"Whoa, what does that mean?" Larry asked with arms so big they stood a foot away from his sides.

"It means that you are doing business with the feds and they marked the deal with my counterfeit money."

Frank got on the phone and called a local number. "The trash has been collected and put out! Yeah," he said, "it was his, and we been sanitized!" Then he stuck the phone at me.

"What would I do if I were you?" I retorted. "I'd pack my bags, cut my losses, try and figure what new guy I got it from, and who pulled them in. Get out of town and time is not on your side," and then I handed the phone off to Larry.

Frank said, "You want a ride back to your car?"

"Just take me to the closest restaurant and drop me off!" The sun was up and it was going to be a nice crisp San Francisco December day. My mouth felt like a welfare family just moved out. My stomach felt like I was making concrete and somebody forgot to add the water. I started for a table to sit down when I noticed a phone and called a cab. I did that about three times before I arrived back to my car on Blacow just about nine A.M.

When I arrived back at the house, I found Diane sitting on the bed with her box of bills and her checkbook, just like time had stopped in that room. "Wanna go to breakfast, babe," I said with a smile big enough for politics.

When the weekend arrived, it had already been raining for five days. The kids who lived in the whole court were driving their moms crazy. Diane put the word out to the neighborhood for a McDonald's play day picnic.

At just about noon on Saturday three fully loaded vans and about six adults—five moms and me—headed off to the local Mickie Dee's.

I knew that the neighborhood had a pretty good idea what I was all about. One of them was being paid nine hundred dollars a month for the feds to park a motor home in their driveway.

As Diane and I stood at the front ordering and paying for everything, Diane noticed that there was a photocopy of a hundred dollar bill hanging on a string so everyone could see it. Diane tipped her head over toward me as she peered over her shoulder at the four mothers standing behind us. She whispered, "Is that one of yours?"

I was absolutely sure it was one of mine but "No," I said. "I cannot tell from here," trying to whisper in her ear and see if we had aroused any curiosity with our dining guests. They seemed more aware of what was going on than I did as they stood there snickering into their hands.

Diane said to the cashier, "Hey, let me see that flyer!"

"Sure," the cashier said. Then as if she had never done it before, she unclipped the flyer and handed it to Diane.

Diane held it close to her breasts, as I looked down I saw my hundred dollar bill, the ones that were printed on the mis-cut watermarked stock. The photocopy was of an un-numbered J series bill. Diane handed it back to the girl and said, "Who brought this in?"

"I dunno," the girl replied.

"How come there is no serial number?" I asked.

"I dunno," the girl replied.

Well, it was McDonald's and it was the closest McDonald's to Diane's house.

*I do not understand what the feds are doing. Why are they going out of their way to let you know they are using your money?*

It left me with nothing but speculation. I had no idea what the feds had in mind for the largest amount of counterfeit in more than twenty-five years. The feds deciding to use your money before they put you in prison, to my knowledge, had never been done before. I had never heard a story in prison that played like this one.

If you got a federal prison with nine hundred men in it, you might have two counterfeiters, hundreds of bank robbers, hundreds of drug dealers, financial fraud, and illegal aliens being held as evidence, but never more than one or two counterfeiters.

I was a little distracted by my own thoughts until Diane said, "I brought you here because we were entertaining the neighborhood kids."

She was right. Obsessing about it was not solving a thing. That dark cloud began to fade away. It was now time for Kimberly's annual Christmas party. I took a Cougar full of just barely teenagers down to the store to pick up party stuff. It was raining that soft chilled misty rain that gives the Bay Area that sensual, sexy atmosphere, all damp and slippery, perfect for fireplace snuggling. I did not know it at the time, but destiny was logging an event into my present, like a time traveler came and gave me a message I did not understand. However it was information that I desperately needed to know.

While I waited for the kids to pick out their stuff so I could pay for it, I was compelled to do something I never do. I grabbed a newspaper off the rack. So why did I open it to about the middle and fold it back? There in the middle of the page was a picture of a black Mercedes being hauled out of the bay at Sausalito by its rear bumper. I got into my car and turned on the interior light. The caption under the picture told me everything I needed to know. The undercover DEA agent in the driver's seat and a recently released inmate in the passenger seat, with one bullet hole in the back of the head each. Five will get you ten that the recently released inmate was let out unexpectedly early. It's one thing to know that you shot a friend in the gut with a dum-dum. It's quite different knowing you made the tip that got two people hit, even if they both had earned it.

*How can you say they both deserved to die when one of them was just doing his job?*

Undercover agents commit crime the same way, for the same reason the criminal does, and there is no honor in that. There is nothing honorable about law enforcement officers pretending to be criminals when you take into account that when he or she sells drugs, people die just like they do when the criminal sells it. Besides, sixty-five percent of all the drugs sold to your children comes directly or indirectly from those slime ball undercover heroes you hold in such high regard. The real players do not sell to kids, they do not sell to those who do. The real players have kids in your schools. They love and protect them just the same and perhaps do a better job than you do. Then they put your kid in prison because the undercover cop, using unlimited tax dollars, tricked your minor child into breaking the law. Then they deny them a fair trial under juvenile law. Who let whom down?

It cracks me up sometimes when I hear those self-righteous accuse the criminal or the outlaw of trying to do it the easy way because we are too lazy to do it the way they did it. Easy never was a part of it. Lazy begins with career government jobs, security guards and ends with the pimp. Everything else takes more self-motivation than most CEOs are required to have. Most federal crime is really nothing evil at all. It is business that is being transacted that does not serve the government or those major players the government pays homage to (i.e., petroleum, pharmaceuticals, and banking). Try to find a federal law that does not restrict trade and business or depletes our undeniable right to life, liberty, and the pursuit of safety and security (i.e., happiness).

That is the reality that separates the world you live in from the world I live in. So is it the lawmakers or the lawbreakers who are to be held responsible for the rise in crime every time the Republicans have control? The reason they need to hire the justices they hire is because the good justices are the ones the Republicans discredit with ambiguous stereotyping. Just once really listen to those debates. If any of it were even close to the truth, the ones who lost in the process would have to be disbarred or hung for treason.

If everyone had been taught flim-flam in high school, the government would have to work a lot harder just to pull the wool over your eyes.

I was beginning to feel like the man with a life-threatening condition and I just lost my hospitalization coverage. It was not so much that I was being set up for another beef as I was being locked into one of the biggest drug stings ever.

They wanted me to be taken out by my own people just for security reasons. They wanted me to need their protection. My name is my product and my product was to be used on a lot of high-profile cases. I would either get hit on the streets or after I go to the slammer.

However that was their plan, and we all know how successful Republican plans are. You remember they were going to kill a president and no one would ever catch on! Then they did it repeatedly until the Kennedys stopped running for president.

*Who? They? You make the whole thing seem like some five-dimensional Parker Brothers game! Every move is a roll of the dice. Your world does not seem very nice and certainly no fun.*

Fun, like chess is fun. It's one on one, and in my world, I directly affect my destiny in much the same way a man in a canoe controls his course with his paddle in a fast-moving current. No matter how hard you paddle, you are going down the river. You just do not have to hit all of the rocks and snags along the way.

However on your side of the law, most of the rocks and nearly all of the snags are put there for you to hit. Dodging some of those rocks and snags is against the law and there are a lot of rules on how you may dodge the rocks and snags.

*Aren't you just venting your own rebellious attitudes in an attempt to justify your self-serving criminal behavior?*

Just think how much better off the farmers and textile workers would be if the government had not made growing hemp illegal just to keep a medicinal herb out of the hands of educated people, the plant from which this country was built and today produces forty thousand products in the United States. However growing it in the United States is against the law, just to prevent an herb that has never killed a single soul from being consumed, an herb that has proof of improving and prolonging life for the people without government healthcare in a country that makes compassionate termination of life illegal while the government snivels about a twenty percent trade deficit and its inability to provide medication for the elderly. How is that law not in contradiction with everything that both parties preach to at every election?

That is reality, and that is why I will be an outlaw for as long as there are laws without sense or authority and people stupid enough to think they have to obey them. If you do not play, there is no game. Jury trials were given to us for the purposes of overthrowing the unlawful laws set upon us by our ill-gotten Congress. Congress does not recognize the herb from the book of Genesis, however juries may only use common sense when deciding a case.

They started the big drug busts in the Bay Area, with the counterfeit being used for the purpose of tracking throughout the drug trade network. From the street to the mother ship and back again. It was just too bad that they let me see it first. No one that was connected to anyone I knew with half a brain got popped with trace money.

Emotionally I survived Christmas and right after Christmas, Diane and I took the children, hers and mine, to Reno, Tahoe, for New Years. I was looking through the sideview mirror of Diane's show van, "Night Moves," when we crossed the state line into Nevada.

Diane looked over at me and said, "None of them turned around and went back. It must be okay to leave the state on federal court probation. See, I told you they loved you, babe," she said as she came over to the driver's seat and did some things I really was not used to in front of my very opinionated young daughter. My boys and Diane's girls thought it was great. Dean and Tracy thought it was sick. Any first year physiologist could have told you that before it happened.

I just figure that one of them is going to need to use me as an example to justify their actions in the future and the others will employ it as a lesson to learn from. Just doing what I can to make life easier for my children. I'm one of those people that happens to think that all of life's lessons are of value or they would not have been put in the book of life. I expect my children to be better people than their parents were. That is the process by which humankind improves themselves, the studies prove it.

Governments, however, almost never improve themselves. Disaster and wars are the only things that change government. We learned decades ago that beating our kids senseless to get them to behave was counterproductive.

When will our government learn that war no longer solves problems, neither do suppressive laws. War creates problems universally and affects the wealthy in the pocketbook and the families of the taxpayers through the loss of family members. Suppressive laws produce a dependant society, while killing enthusiasm for self-sufficiency, just like a dictatorship, and is treason under our founding documents.

Read your history and you will find out who has which plan for America. Then check the economic history for the last fifty years. You will find that the facts contradict the redirect of the pseudo-intellectual political analysts.

It was time to go and receive my sentence. I loved my new life with Diane; she was the other side of me that I never knew. I'd come to love her children. Even so, doing it made me have guilt because my time was split between her kids and mine. I kept trying to think of a way that Diane and I could have met other than the way it happened so that my leaving her would not have ever been required. Logic told me that Diane was part of this path and any other path would have never crossed hers.

I had not involved Diane in any of the hearings up until now. I was not sure that her being there now was going to help ease the pain or make it worse. We parked the van in the same lot that I used every time before. It was a bit of a walk to the courthouse, but it was the easiest and quickest point of departure.

We waited and then we waited some more. Bogart got sentenced first. Boy, was that good news. He got five years probation of a sort that if he failed on the last day, Judge Laughlin E. Waters would call him back and make him serve the whole five years the hard way.

Then it was my time. The judge seemed to have some big grudge against me, or he was pissed that I had not had my lawyer deliver an offering unto him, as he knew my bond was worth fifty thousand dollars and it was cash. My sentence was the maximum allowed under the single indictment rule covered by a disparity of sentencing order of law. The same rule that kept me from copping to the lowest time charge was the same rule that kept him from giving me substantially more time than any other defendant under the single indictment. They outwitted themselves again.

It went something like this: six years in a maximum security prison with absolutely no community programs versus Bogart's reporting to a probation officer once a month for five years and piss testing to make sure that there was no counterfeit money in his urine.

It was less then ten years and I got the judge to give me a self-committal stay of execution. Yes, by law, under bond, if you made all your court dates and got nothing, not even a parking ticket, then the court has no justification to deny a self-committal request. That meant I stayed on the street until the Federal Bureau of Prisons decided where, quite literally in hell, I would be doing my time.

Fat chance in hell—if the feds did not want me on the street, the judge would have said no. Now you know why the judge was so tight-jawed through the whole hearing—not because I was a turn-around counterfeiter doing a back-to-back beef. Judge Waters was an old, senile, Republican appointee judge who had out priced his worth to anyone, including an airline suit on whose fault it was if the interior of an airplane combusts and who should pay passenger claims.

Judge Waters put it up for bid right in court, mumbling to the two teams of lawyers, "No one has yet presented me with anything worthy of a ruling either way," and closing with, "The first one who comes to me with something worth considering will win my ruling." Was that judge ruling or judge drooling!

I was honored to turn and walk out of the courtroom, filled to capacity with federal agents. Diane arose from her seat on the aisle in the middle of the court. I paused to take her by the arm and walked out.

While we waited for our lawyers to do the courtroom paper shuffle, there we stood; Bogart and his very beautiful show girl lawyer standing on one side of the foyer with an almost attractive FBI agent or U.S.-less marshal.

On the other side of the room was me and Diane in her stiletto heals and her dagger red lips and nails.

*What were you thinking at that very moment?*

What I was thinking right at that moment was, *I'm going home until the sixth of February 1981.* The only other thing that I could think was that if you added the one to ten scores of Bogart's two females together, Diane had them

71

beat cold at better than ten to one. She was more than just beautiful; she was intelligent, armed, and beautiful. It was a good thing that no children were present when two poorly dressed U.S. marshals came over and stood in front of us.

"Jennings," a faceless marshal said in a resentful tone, "because you decided not to co-operate with us and tell us everything we know you know about the whereabouts of Christopher Boyce, we are going to turn that little bit of time the judge just gave you into a death sentence. You have been there, you know firsthand nobody dies in federal prison we don't want to die. How many people did you see die the last time you were down, Jennings? Or you could change your mind, it's still not too late to change your mind!"

I did have a memory all right. I was waiting outside the gate at Lompoc Maximum Security Prison when they pulled a man through the gate on a stretcher covered with a sheet up to his neck that had more bloodstains on it than I could count. As the screws loaded the nearly dead inmate into the Vandenburg ambulance, the guards were on the radio taking bets on whether or not the prisoner would live long enough to get to the air base hospital. They were making sport of a man's life as if it were a football game. When they gestured me to enter, I refused and returned to my dorm. Warden Taylor asked why I did not come in to do the printing. I told him that I would not return to work if the inmate died. He did and I didn't!

"It will never be too late for my whole sentence, asshole, 'cause that's how long it's going to take you dumb asses to find him." Boy that felt good—six years good. Not quite, but it would have to do.

Meanwhile the other faceless fool who was standing excessively closer to Diane than good common sense would dictate laughed down at her!

Diane grabbed his necktie about in the middle and stabbed one stiletto heel into his foot. "You know what, motherfucker," Diane snarled up into his face, "I'm going to take him home and fuck his brains out and you ain't got nobody who will ever do that for you except maybe your mother! When February sixth comes around, he will be begging to go to prison so he can get some rest. What do you think about that, asshole?"

I had all the reason I would ever need to love her for the rest of my life. Just when I thought it could not get any better, she grabbed me by the hand and dragged me across the room. Then when she was right in Bogart's face, while she held me behind her, she said, "I should cut off your dick and balls; you ain't got no business having anything that belongs to a man."

The look on the women's faces was a big bonus from just a moment before but when I noticed that both women moved just a little bit away from Bogart that was chocolate cake. That spoke volumes on how they really felt about the man they were schmoozing with just moments earlier.

As soon as I had my walking papers, we did just that. Diane hailed a cab and we headed in the opposite direction than the car was at. Once the cabby understood our motive, things really took off with more creativity than the job really required. I gave him a fifty and thanked him for a five-minute ride I would not forget soon!

Reality was setting in; choices had to be made that were going to be final. We went to Zuba's house to collect Kimberly, Dean, and Sonya. I had all I could do just to maintain my composure. I did not want to visit with my friends and I did not want to meet any of Diane's friends either.

Diane was trying hard to operate around my dark mood. I just knew that I had one month left, and I did not want to do it in the dumps. The dumbest thing I ever said to her was she did not know what I was going through.

# Chapter Nine
# Of the Second Part

*In my heart,* the only thing I wanted to do was disappear. The easiest thing for me to do would be to just disappear. There was a boat in a Bay Area marina large enough to take both families to another country. I had loaded it out myself. If I ran, I would run alone.

*Why would you run alone? Why would you not take Diane and your kids and hers with you?*

Diane told me early on that she would gladly follow me to the ends of the earth and never look back if it were not for the fact that she had children she could not leave behind or take with us. Her face told me how real that was for both of us.

If I ran and got busted right away or ten years down the road, my time would at least double. The way I feel about my children and Diane and her children would not allow me to voluntarily leave and not come back. If I were to take one or all, they would be in violation of the law. If I were to go and the feds got close, I must be willing to kill and/or die rather than be captured. For me, I had no problem with that. Prison was a known factor and that was the biggest reason for making the run.

*I do not understand. You seemed to be having such a great time at Camp Lompoc. Tractors, trucks, and marijuana more readily available than in Humbolt County. Now you act like it is an intolerable alternative. You got what you wanted, less than ten years.*

Contrary to the Bobbie Gentry's lyric, "Freedom's just another word for nothing left to lose," prison is just another word for nothing left to lose. Freedom is the word for everything and nothing more to need.

Adventure had been my life, my whole life; my marriage did not survive that addiction. It was not likely that I would be allowed back into a camp. Especially as the judge had overstepped his authority in mandating maximum security, not his decision! The judge gives you the time, it is up to the Federal Bureau of Prisons how you do that time. This alone could be reason enough to overturn his sentence, Laughlin's way of putting his hand out for a modification of sentence embracery. That had nothing to do with why I was apprehensive about going back to prison. I had a gut feeling that somehow there was something more going on that I was not yet aware of. The unknown factor!

Premonitions: I had a dream in the navy that my term of enlistment was up and they did not let me out. Then when I had less than a month to go I got extended for the Vietnam War. I had a dream before I got sentenced that my sentence was over by a year and they were not going to let me out. Premonition or future knowledge?

The days disappeared faster than cookies from a cookie jar. I knew that I would get weak if I stayed to the end. I hoped Diane would understand why I just slipped over the back fence on the first of February and hitched a ride in a red Mustang.

It was going to take me six days and fifteen hundred miles by myself to get ready to turn myself in to do what would turn out to be 95 percent of six years. I had no idea that every trucker I hitched with was wanting to run me across an international border. All I had to do was call it—heads, Canada; tails, Mexico. Jenningses have been running to Canada and Mexico ever since the king sent us over here in the custody of the Leighs to settle Virginia.

The only thing I was worrying about was that twenty-twenty hindsight once I arrived in Springfield, Missouri. Oh, how I hate always being right and not knowing it until it's too late.

The morning of the sixth of February at 11:45 A.M., I arrived at the federal equivalent of Amityville. It had all the charm and beauty of the Bates Motel. Built over one hundred years ago as an insane asylum for the State of Missouri, then sold to the federal government, the founding charter for the Federal Bureau of Prison states that it was "created for the purpose of incarceration of individuals who have violated federal law and *for other reasons*." They never defined what these other reasons are in that charter.

All I know is I'm one of the other people that is there for one of those other reasons. If I did not believe it then, I was going to believe it very soon.

The feds never saw me leave. The U.S.-less marshals were in the court right out front of Diane's house on February sixth at twelve noon, central time,1981. Actually they had been there since the judge gave me self-committal a month earlier. More precisely the feds had been using the court as a staging area since the day Diane brought me home from the airport. That is why they wanted me to get the Cougar back. That way they did not have to learn and memorize a new plate number.

Diane was getting ready to go to her store when the marshals brought about fifty guns to bear.

"Freeze!"

They almost stopped Diane's poor little heart as she was bending to unlock her gold Cadillac Bertz. Knowing her the way I do, she would recover real quick and let them know they pulled iron on the wrong chick!

I was half-naked, standing in front of the receiving screw's desk when the phone rang.

"Yes, this is central receiving," the fat tax burner replied. "Yeah, I'm processing him in right now," he said, leaning back in his chair with ease as his ass was the heaviest object in this hemisphere.

"Of course, I'm sure it's Jennings," he said as he shuffled through the papers on his desk until he found the one he had clipped my driver's license onto.

"When I punched Jennings's California driver's license number into the computer it came up with his federal number. What, you think someone else would be turning himself in for Jennings? I know we are out here in the farm belt and that we're not as sharp as you west coast marshals.

"I guess you should have told the agents staking out your old lady's house that you were leaving," he said as he hung up the phone. "How long ago did you leave?"

"Yesterday," I replied. "I left yesterday," *and I'll be home tomorrow*, I added under my breath. Now all I had to do was make all of the days in between yesterday and tomorrow disappear. It's called mind over matter. As long as you have a good mind, it does not matter.

The first few weeks are tough and the blues hang out a lot longer where the trees and the skies are all gray, day after day. Even the snow had dirty specks in it that would turn into brown slush as the days went slowly by.

I wasn't on the floor and in my dorm one hot New York minute when an inmate rolled up on me. "You the counterfeiter," he said, looking at me like he would love to rip open my throat.

Returning the look, I replied, "Yeah!"

The inmate threw a note on my bunk and said, "Read it," then he turned and left.

It appeared that I had been pre-registered with the welcome wagon. Following the directions in the note I found my way to the part of the prison where the politically well-connected got to stay while taking a sabbatical from the family's business. It takes a lot of political clout to have a private room in this federal joint. Where I ended up was not a private room, it was more like a private suite of rooms. The large man in his bathrobe and slippers never rose from where he was splayed out in his kitchen chair with one foot draped over the corner of the '50s styled table, dangling his slipper from his toe.

He and his resident houseboy and card player were engaged in a card game when I knocked on the door jamb. I now understood why the note guy was so pissed, thinking maybe I would replace him on the "A" deck of the good ship lock-up.

Barely looking up from his hand, the large man with the big neck and a last name that ended with a vowel pointed to a large double door locker and said, "Help yourself to what ever you need."

Before I could utter a word he continued, "Don't be bashful, take as much of whatever you want. It's all being taken care of."

As I got ready to leave, looking like a kid carrying cordwood, I attempted to thank him.

"No need to thank me," still acting like he was attempting to shoe a pesky fly away. "I'm just doing a favor for a friend of a friend. You don't have to pay me back and you don't have to be my best friend. So just pretend you do not know me should you see me again outside this room. If you encounter any problems you cannot resolve with the inmates or staff on your own, see my man," he said diverting his eyes from me to the young inmate seated across from him with both feet draped over the other corner of the red and chrome table.

When I re-entered the fifty-seven-man dorm where I was the only white person, I got the feeling that any trouble anyone was planning just got canceled. As secret as our meeting may have been, short of a memo on the warden's desk, my back was covered with a power from above. In this case, I mean the third floor!

Springfield, Missouri Federal Prison was the scariest place I ever had to live. It is more than a prison, it is three separate prisons in one. The buildings are connected by an underground tunnel.

One building houses a complete hospital, with doctors and nurses. No longer would I wonder what happened to Hitler's medical experiments. There were hideous abnormalities that if you were to see them in a black and white movie you would laugh at the preposterous imagination of the screenwriter.

Prisoners with claws coming out of their toes and sometimes their fingers just below the fingernail or where the nail should have been. They appeared to be coming from a bone in the last joint. There were others with very webbed fingers and toes. Those were the birth defects I had never seen before. They were not without the birth defects we are all familiar with, like six toes, six fingers, and stubby hairy tails.

The doctors were all graduates of the "Hide and Jeckle Medical University of Midevilisum" and hand-selected by the number of malpractice cases they had lost to be nominated for this prestigious appointment.

Before I am accused of having an overactive imagination, visualize this: You have a patient and it has been determined that both feet have to be amputated. Would you make both stubs the same length, or would you do what the federal prison doctors decided to do and have a four-inch difference between the ends of the two stubs?

Sherlock, the famous Belton Bandit, my new confidant, and I concluded that if he were to escape it would be easier for the U.S. marshals to track him in the snow or the mud.

Sherlock and I worked on the same crew; we both did so to get access to the majority of the prison. We were both jailhouse lawyers and pragmatic thinkers and planners. We did not do a lot of sitting around and chatting. When we talked, it was for the purpose of transmitting information about the things we were both predisposed to seek out and know. A man who goes to prison and forgets that he is still an outlaw gets out of prison a beaten-down loser.

Continuing down the underground corridor was a mental hospital with the same high quality of staff appointments, the warden in charge of the better mental health through enhanced drugs. Once again let me point out that I came to that conclusion on the day that Sherlock and I gained access to the head shrink's/warden's office when it was not otherwise occupied.

Spring was coming and we needed to balance the individual heating and cooling units and change the filters. On the desk sat a coffee cup from a drug company awarding him the honor of being the largest purchaser of Thorazine in the entire nation.

We took turns rifling the offices for anything we could use against them for leverage in ways they could never figure out. It was like espionage, it was like practice. Kind of like weight lifters and piano players—you have to do it regularly or lose the edge.

We were both jacketed by the feds as conmen and manipulators. So we did know what we were shopping for. We just found more fraud than good common sense would allow one to believe. The biggest crooks in the prison system are not the inmates and we uncovered the paper work that proved it.

We concluded that he had received considerably more than just a coffee cup by the way he order enough stuff, according to Sherlock, to make a street dealer very wealthy and keep him that way for life. That was the day I saw the Thorazine shuffle as narrated by Sherlock!

*THE BELL RANG AND THE DOORS OPENED AND INMATES CAME SLIDE FOOT'N DOWN THE HALL. MEET WILLIAM JENNINGS—HE FELL ASLEEP ON AN EAST-BOUND GREYHOUND BUS! WHEN HE AWOKE HE WAS HERE, A KIND OF HELL IN WHICH EVERY-ONE BUT HE HAD RESIGNED THEMSELVES TO THIS MINDLESSNESS TO ESCAPE THE INESCAPABLE MADNESS OF MONOTONY IN A BLEAK EXISTENCE OF VIEWING THE WORLD THROUGH TINY BOXES. WELCOME, MR. JENNINGS, TO THE THORAZINE ZONE.*

A shuddering chill rippled through my body as the big steel doors closed behind us as we continued on our circular daily journey that ended back in the third part of the prison, the part of the prison that housed the inmates and workshops that maintained the entire prison.

My mother always said that a rose by any other name would still smell as sweet. Ergo a one-hundred-year-old insane asylum by any other name is still just as chilling. Especially at night when you could never be sure that the sounds you heard were of the present, the past, or your screams echoing back from your future.

Take into account that most of the inmates migrated regularly from one part of the prison to the other as residents. Just because they were not in the nuthouse did not mean they were not nuts and we just did not know for sure that any or all of the Thorazine Team had ever had a problem of the mind to begin with.

Sherlock and I were sure about one thing—the inmate who broke his leg in the wood factory, which resulted in having his broken leg removed because it did not heal right, when he gets out of prison next year, he will no longer be known as the fleet-footed bank robber.

If you desire drugs and you have no regard other than assuring that you will be stupid stoned, then Springfield, Missouri, is your Alameda, where all you have to say is, "I cannot sleep. Can you give me something?" A few more months and you will be cruising your way to the chemical lobotomy known as the "Thorazine Shuffle!"

A safe bet would be 99 percent just wanted a good night's sleep in a very creepy place that seemed to have a troubled spirit of its own, where ghostly horror walked the halls at night, every night.

The biggest mistake I made was allowing the hospital to follow up on the heart attack I'd had in the navy, the final straw that started me down this road in the first place. One day I appeared on the hospital call-out sheet. It took the doctor about ten minutes and he had concluded that my heart problem could be solved with just a simple operation. Then he stuck me in a room with a movie projector and a 1957 black and white Gulf Oil film about the operation the doctor wanted to perform.

Like seeing a man cut with a meat and bone saw from his neck bone to his belly, then spread open with this tool that looked like a big shiny bear trap, was going to win my approval. If I had been suicidal, this was my way out, with a nice law suit settlement for my family. Most families do not know what they could receive with the right lawyer. If you were ever lucky enough to have had a relative that died at Springfield, Missouri Federal Prison, I know the lawyer you need to call.

Thinking is what you have a million dollars worth of in prison per year. Don't leave without first using up all of your thinking time, or you will have to come back and use it up later. Thinking that requires getting to a certain place.

"Hey, new fish," Sherlock called out with a grin on his face that gave me reason to think that he either wanted to kiss me or he wanted to share the air in the shower with a roach, the kind you roll and burn.

I do not care what any of you Midwesterners claim, your weed sucks—no, really. It's not hay you shouldn't need a bale just to get heady. Half of the dorm rushed into the shower as we walked out.

I flung myself down on my bed and looked up at the ceiling so I could escape into a time and place back when this ceiling was built.

"Did you ever think for a minute that just perhaps it's the man carrying out their death sentence," Sherlock shouted from the corner of my mind. "Did they not say that they were going to turn that six into life, which is just another word for death."

"Damn, Sherlock, I want to buy that cow pasture!"

"What pasture? I cut it with a little bit of opium!"

"Yeah and this was like a warning. We can stop your heart anytime we want to," I concluded.

"Plus you know the navy gave them that nervous breakdown you had coming out of combat your last west pac! I'll watch your back, but in here that can get you a tranquilizer in the ass, your hands tied to the fence with two bullets in the back as soon as the drugs wear off enough to pass the death certificate," Sherlock added with a twist of his head as he sat in the chair by my bunk.

"Other reason is they got me down for helping Boyce escape," I said, blowing out a big breath, making my mind spin out of control.

"At a time like this," Sherlock interjected, "normally I would tell somebody like you that I would swap jackets with them. Woo, noo, wayyy I want in your jacket, Jennings. My time seems fine, five to fifteen you can take to the bank, if you know what I mean," and we both laughed much more than called for.

The next day Sherlock was called out. Seemed his annual chest x-ray had a spot on it and they wanted to rip his chest open and rip out his lung and save his life.

"Please, Doctor!" Sherlock screamed. "Please let me die on the table, Doc! Promise me, Doc, life is just not worth living as half a man. I would pass out just oxygenating enough blood for a good hard-on!"

In Springfield, Missouri Federal Prison, sign no blank forms or you will end up on the table with a doctor that has a Ph.D. in ops. Welcome to the land of the living cadavers. Try to tell anyone on the outside, you'll end up doing the Thorazine Shuffle. It did not take long for these two conmen to figure the game in this bag. Halloween on Elm Street is just one day a year; every day is Halloween here at this Club Fed.

It was no accident that they sent me to this prison halfway across the United States, instead of the institution closest to the inmate's release destination as called for in prison policy "fifty one hundred point one." So as a master manipulator being manipulated outside the guidelines of the Federal Bureau of Prisons, it was my obligation to outmanipulate the collective intelligence of the finest, most sophisticated group of federal enforcement professionals in the history of this nation according to your president. Only one rule applied—they have total control of everything; they own the key.

The reality that all of what I was doing seemed less like my plan and more like their plan for me. The other possibility is Destiny, because divine intervention just flunked the logic test. It was time to do an inspection of the facts. Sherlock and I were going into the hospital and securing anything that we can use as a stay out of surgery guarantee clause.

It was a sure bet that if the government needed information, that would mean they needed you living to get it. It was also a sure bet that if they put you under for surgery, they could get it while you are out.

I needed to get out of this prison or I would not live long enough to figure out why they were so pissed about the counterfeit, or was it the Boyce thing? The possibility that it could have something to do with things that had not happened yet never occurred to me.

*Impossible* in my dictionary has only one definition: "Has not yet been attempted by a Jennings!" If you think I'm being boastful, you have not been keeping score. From the moment the United States Navy defrauded my contract and refused to release me from my re-enlistment, I threw away a lot of rules I used to live by. In time, you lose respect for them when you find that you are not the only one they screw over and over again. Unfortunately most of the injured are shamed out of waging a complaint. From this the federal government takes justification for their acts of treachery against there most dedicated citizens, the military veterans!

Disgruntled is the term used to describe people who do something disgustingly unexcitable in retaliation for what the government said is just an unfortunate misunderstanding. You know, like Waco was the result of Janet Reno misunderstanding the Constitution and her authority while overstepping both. Dead people do not complain or sue, and they shame the living from speaking out for the sinners who were killed under violations of constitutional law.

Where is it written that Christians cannot arm themselves for Armageddon? Does the government have constitutional authority to disarm a Christian body on their own compound? However no one weeps for Waco, no one wants to understand the truth about the lie that day created.

These are the reasons that Sherlock and I were comfortable knowing even if he had a speck on his lung and I have a problem with my heart requiring surgery, this place was the best reason to not go under the knife.

One day shortly after arriving, I remember telling Sherlock in chow line that being there was a complete dental facility capable of turning out their own dental hardware, I should get my teeth done for free and save a lot of money when I get out.

Sherlock started swatting me with his tray until this big Hawaiian-looking inmate wearing a green dental smock turned around and said, "I'd think it over if I were you. Six inmates died in dental in the last four months."

"What about getting your teeth clean? That can't kill you," I begged.

"Two of them were teeth cleanings." The big Hawaiian shrugged.

"How in hell do they kill you while cleaning your teeth?" I challenged.

"The doctor went off to take a phone call and left the gas on for twenty minutes. They wrote it off as an inmate OD!"

"Why was he even taking gas for a teeth cleaning?" me, not being a junkie, asked.

"Ironically because the doctor needed to hone his skills putting people under and the inmate volunteered to get high. He had six months left on a dime," the Hawaiian added as he turned and placed his tray on the rail of the food service bar.

Hoping for just an ounce of justice, I asked, "What was he doing time for?" hoping that on a moral level he had it coming.

"They kept him in the nut ward for eight of the ten because he believed that the CIA funded 90 percent of all the terrorist acts committed in the world and I guess he tried to prove it," said the Hawaiian as he offered us the opportunity to join him for lunch.

"Don't tell me—disgruntled Vietnam Vet, and he was trained in demolition, that and the truth got him eliminated!"

I quickly learned that you are not safe by not going to the doctor here. When they want you they come and get you with about six guards and one hypodermic. After you see it happen a half-dozen times the more obvious it becomes. Just like the movie *Conspiracy Theory* blended with *One Flew over the Cuckoo's Nest* only without all the magic of Hollywood to make it come out all right for the Cids.

However when you meet people like James Fenamore Cooper still doing time, walking the yard with the Texas Chainsaw Massacre killer and this old Indian who literally ate his entire family, a place where these guys walk the yard in general population, you soon believe every prison horror show you have ever seen. This is not the dark ages, it's the '80s and the Republicans have been running the game long enough to fix it if they had a mind to do so, or were they the ones that created it?

# CHAPTER TEN

*If you are* not living on the edge, you do not have the best view. Sherlock and I put our heads together. The big question was what could I have that they wanted that was more valuable than their desire to kill me? Part two, did the government want the information and then they would eliminate me after they had it or was it just the information they wanted?

Part three, how do I win? If I had known the future then I could not have made a better plan than the one I did on that cold day in March.

Step one, I must take control of the game by going out in front of the sharks and get in the water. You can learn a lot by listening to the post-Vietnam era songs. Then lay the bait where they must access it illegally, tell a story so compelling with just enough innuendo in it to let those in the know believe I knew more than I had admitted to in the past and title it "Where the Falcon Flies Free" and end it with "please, dear God, do not forget about me."

So putting pencil to paper, I began to write a story for the media, most specifically Robert Lindsey, whom at this time was in the Bay Area. As the feds were delaying my mail while every agency read my incoming and outgoing mail, a letter to Lindsey would ring the bells of the two competing federal agencies and arouse the sleeping dogs of the CIA.

*Why the author of* Flight of the Falcon? *Was it because he was in the Bay Area or just because he would have the most to gain from having the story first?*

Lindsey was the last person that wanted to read the story I wrote as he had to agree to never tell the whole truth about what it really was that Chris was doing and why. He was forced to write less than the truth in his second book, *Flight of the Falcon.*

However the repeated ambiguous statement that the feds were too stupid to edit out of the story. This would make anything I say seem plausible, probable, and circumstantially provable.

*What ambiguous statement would that be?*

Lindsey wrote on a number of occasions, as did the screenwriter, that Boyce stated to the Snowman, AKA Dalton Lee, "You don't understand what they are doing," and variations on that theme appeared throughout the books and the movie that referred to the power structure in Washington, D.C., the things they were really doing while telling the world that they were not doing it.

*What things are you talking about?*

What if Boyce had not become a spy? You talk about a scenario for a time travel movie, imagine if Christopher Boyce never got the job at TRW— talk about a paradox!

The true intellect would have to question, the question, which never answered itself. Writers pose questions for two reasons, as Lindsey never put an answer to that question then he used it for only one reason. It was the answer and the reason for everything.

There was a truth to Boyce's action that if known to the world would justify his act of espionage. This secret, if known, would bring controversy to the "Salt Talks" of the '70s. The question, if answered, would prove Reagan to be a fool or a liar or both. A choice between those two would not sit well with the people of either party.

Having the answer made it obvious to the major players that the plan was to provoke the Soviets and would guarantee a nuclear war and although we would have prevailed as winners, the collateral damage throughout the world would change everything, making all of the living dependant on a strictly controlled government under a single world leadership. Kind of like the plan that Bush had when he replaced Ronnie.

That's why Lindsey is held under an illegal non-disclosure agreement that forbids any contact between Lindsey; Bob Martin AKA Brent Pope AKA Lynn Dale Bogart; Larry Harold Smith AKA Big Larry AKA William Brian Jennings AKA Hundred Dollar Bill; the Snowman AKA Dalton Lee and perhaps several others unknown to me.

*How do you know this is true? How could you prove it was true, as what you allege did not happen because Boyce did work at TRW?*

"The proof is in the pudding" is an old saying that makes sense if you think about how pudding becomes pudding. Set a question on the shelf and let it set undisturbed and it, like pudding, will prove it self. If that does not get it for you then perhaps you will follow the bird of like feathers, just to see if it waddles and quacks. Does the tail ever wag the dog? Can you tell just by looking?

Just like Forrest Gump and his box of chocolate, when you fish you never know what you are going to hook. It took about two weeks for a strike on the bait. Some poor schmuck ended up in the morgue, and I ended up in the hole sitting on a murder charge and nobody even told me that for over fifteen days. I had not wasted my time, I read the entire New Testament cover to cover with just a forty watt bulb in a fourteen-foot ceiling while sitting on a cold concrete floor. Scripture helps when you are doing battle with the dark side, Grasshopper.

Then I told the screw I wanted to talk to the FBI. The next day they arrived right after breakfast. I was taken to a real nice interview room where they kept the supplies for this wing of the institution. They were nice enough to provide one of those federal wooden chairs for me to sit on in handcuffs.

"What's on your mind, William? Is William okay or do you prefer Bill?" asked the one that was clearly the tallest and wearing the latest style Botany 500.

"Mr. Jennings works just fine for me, thanks," I said as I straddled the chair backwards, resting my handcuffs on the back of the chair.

"What's on your mind, Mr. Jennings? It's your dime, tell us why we are here," said the shorter, younger, dumber, and wearing someone else's re-tailored Botany 500.

"You are here because you got me stuck here in Satan's bedroom and you are going to get me out and back to the institution closest to my home, Pleasanton or Lompoc Camp. You are going to give me a seven-day furlough transfer, and you are going to pick up the tab."

"If that's what you want, just tell the U.S. marshals. You are under their jurisdiction," said the tall one who had every reason in the world to think he was the personification of the FBI.

"I would, you see, but I didn't think that Larry Homminick needed any of my help. He told me way back at Lompoc that he didn't need me for anything. He said Boyce was stupid and they would get him real soon."

"Well, Jennings, you're out of luck. We do not need anything you have either," said the subordinate with his pant cuffs sweeping the dust from the floor.

"Now what are you going to do, Mr. Jennings?" said the I-am-too-good-for-Vogue agent as he finally removed his sunglasses in the dimly lit room.

"I guess I will be very highly paid for my little story about the Falcon," I said as he put his sunglasses carefully into his shirt pocket and extracted my handwritten story in the undelivered envelope addressed to Diane.

"You mean this story, Mr. Jennings? Tell me where do you get this shit that history will prove that Boyce is America's greatest patriot since World War II? Are you on crank, Jennings?"

"You cannot keep that. It is the original uncorrected first draft. It's a collectors item, and it belongs to my estate. The finished draft was read over the phone and recorded by Diane a week before I mailed out the decoy to you."

"Are you saying that your wife has the other copy?" Mr. Cool shot back at me with his finger in my face.

"One of them. By now there are at least a dozen tapes, on Memorex. Anyone listening to it will know it is me, dead or alive," I cast off like this meeting had no purpose. "I just wanted you to know I got around you. The press already knows you want what I got, therefore it must be credible."

"Lindsey got this?" he continued in my face.

"Lindsey already knows it. He wrote the book and talked to Boyce, just like I talked to Boyce. Do you really think that the press will believe you or me?" And the award for best actor goes to?

"We are done here, Jennings. If you had anything you would be begging for a deal. You know how many people want to get Boyce. If we put the word out and you know what we will tell them. You know you are already dead."

"And you captured Chris when?" I taunted at them as they walked away.

I was returned to my cell, knowing that the prison would tell the U.S. marshals that the FBI paid me a visit. The bid has been put on the table and the dogs of war have been set upon it, I reported to Sherlock via the chow cart.

That was a Friday and on Sunday afternoon, the captain of the hole had me delivered to his office for a very strange conversation. "Mr. Jennings, why are you in the hole?"

"I have not a clue, I just thought that this was part of the VIP package," I said in disbelief of his question.

"It says here in your file that you are being held for a murder investigation, but the only dead man I have died while you were on call-out with your boss, so why are you here?" he put to me again.

"So why am I here in your office and your hole, if I did not kill anyone?" I said as the captain racked his fingers over his face.

"Go back to your cell, Jennings, and I will send you back to your dorm either tonight or first thing in the morning," he said, still unable to figure out how he got used.

He seemed to be a man of conscience. The question should have been, What the hell is he doing in purgatory, not why I was there?

The turnkey that returned me to my suite told me on the way that I should roll up and get ready to go back to my dorm.

"What, and give up all of this?" I replied as the screw undid my cuffs through the hole in the door.

As luck would have it, he returned a few minutes later and said, "You ready to go, Mr. Jennings?"

"No, if I go back now I will have to go stand in the chow line. If I get high first I will miss chow altogether!"

"The chow cart is here, so if you want to wait until chow is served I will take you out when I finish passing out the trays. I will give you your tray right now, or do you want to take your shower first?"

*You are making that up or you are just taking literary license? The screws are not stewards, or are they?*

Welcome to Club Fed. The higher the security level the more services they must perform for the inmate. If it were not for the bleak surroundings, one might think they are at Motel 6 with room service. They not only keep the lights on for us they turn them out promptly at ten P.M.

As the shower was not as good as the one in my dorm, I just dined and was escorted back to the security doors. It felt good to be released from jail back to the freedom of prison. I was going to have that feeling many more times as I would do twenty-five percent of a six-year sentence in the hole. That's what happens when a little boy watches *Cool Hand Luke* too many times. It was a good movie and an even better lesson on how will can overcome the insanity of the lowest mentality on earth—prison staff. Walter Winchell said many times that "if one wanted to see the scourge of the earth, just watch the changing of the guard at any federal prison." I am sorry, Walter, nothing has changed in over fifty years.

The prison grapevine had let Sherlock know I was on my way home. "Hey, new fish, want to go share silage?"

"Why, you sweet talk'n bank robber, how did you know what was on my mind?" I said with a wide grin of approval.

"You eat yet?" Sherlock inquired as he put his hand on my shoulder.

"Yeah, sure, of course. Let's burn it and then unroll my bag. I still have a ton of munchies left over from the welcome wagon," I replied as we strolled down to the stairwell and disappeared into the wall.

We had gotten hold of the blueprints as we worked in mechanical services. We had found so many access areas throughout these old buildings that went nowhere. One day we might find one of the five ways out past the fence line. As we sat in the dark smoking, joking, and planning our next play, we could hear the screws trying to figure out where the smell of cannabis was coming from.

When the sound of voices dwindled down we exited the locked access panel and returned to our separate dorms.

The next morning Sherlock said as he handed me my coffee cup from the rack, "You ready to do this?"

I turned as the crew boss rolled up behind us. "You guys ready to go on your rounds?" as he stuck about five pink repair slips into Sherlock's hand.

"No, Boss," I replied. "I have to go see Glover, my case manager."

"You want a walk'n slip, Jennings?"

"Yeah, Boss, it will keep me from having to kill a half-dozen screws just to see my case manager," I replied.

Our boss was a good guy, a Midwest farm boy that had to work at the prison so he could afford to be a farmer. I understood that real well as my dad had to be a shipbuilder so he could afford to be a farmer. It has always amazed me that no one has ever caught on to the fact the government's greatest desire is to destroy the American farm so they can starve the nation into submission. It must be obvious that the politicians all hate farmers. My whole life farmers have been told by the government what they can and cannot do, from where they can sell it and where they may not.

Every four years they get screwed all over again. The proof is the farmers are not any better off today than they were in 1944! Maybe it's time that the farmers tell the government to screw off or they will sell nothing to them. You know, like an embargo against an evil government!

The more the government controls, the more they screw up. These are the same people who declared DDT bad, cranberries cause cancer, eggs will kill you, and milk is bad for your children.

These same mental midgets declared that an herb is a drug, and that the herb, drug, has no medicinal value. Whenever government dictates science the people lose, history screams out that truth. Stem cells are not little people; unlike people stem cells have potential for a more abundant life for the disadvantaged. That is why the government is against it?

I just wish that just one Congressperson would sit down on the toilet and read the dictionary. Just so they could know the definition of an herb and a drug. Now this brain dead knowledge void known as our president and Congress have taken the authority to tell scientists what they may and may not explore. So now we can have a government and scientists who do not serve humanity. Like somehow this will serve humankind, to be the only nation that must clear Congress before we may try something new.

Other countries may not be so mini-minded, so what morality are you saving for this tiny world? What is even dumber is we let them call themselves our leaders. Who needs a leader to stand still or go backwards? They have dictated every aspect of our economy into complete and utter failure. When will the government figure out that war is bad for everything and everybody? Science did not cause war, leaders cause wars so they can be leaders.

# CHAPTER ELEVEN

**Mr. Glover was** not expecting me, as he did not put me on call-out. Glover and I went at each other the first day I arrived here at "Club Fear." So I was looking forward to my little presentation.

*How do you do this? Do you write a script and then just memorize it like a sales pitch?*

I clear my mind of everything except the one thing I want to accomplish. Then I knocked on the door jamb of Glover's office. Glover looked up and waved me in as he was doing something with his hands, therefore he could not speak.

Most prison personnel look like the kind of people you expect to see at the bottom of the well of humanity. He wore a heavy brown tweed suit jacket and brown polyester pants. His expressionless face demonstrated his intellectual awareness.

"Why are you here, Jennings? Whatever it is, I do not have the time. As you can see I am swamped with paperwork."

"This won't take long Glover. All you have to do is call Mr. Phiffler in Washington, D.C. He is the bureau chief of the U.S. marshals."

"What makes you think Phiffler wants to talk to you, Jennings?"

"Right off the bat, that is none of your fucking business!" This is called winning approval.

"Look, Jennings, I could just throw you right back in the fucking hole."

"Yeah, speaking of that, I was there for fifteen days and you never came to see me and I had no team. The next time you break the fucking rules, I'll jam a broken broomstick up your ass. Now dial the fucking telephone!" That's called being assertive and taking control of the negotiations.

*Did you have to be so rude? After all the guy is just doing his job! You claim to be this intellectual but you use vulgarity like it was water.*

He does not have a choice. When an inmate requests to speak to law enforcement, it is his job to facilitate that communication promptly and with security and privacy.

I then closed the door and sat down next to Glover's desk, as he looked through the government green pages. He started to dial the number. "And what do you want me to tell him?" now whispering with the door closed.

It is called playing the game. How many times have you complained when doing your business with the government, and they tell you, you have to play the game! I was just playing the federal prison game. Also, let me point out that a truly intelligent person knows how to communicate at all levels of humanity. Communication no matter how perfectly proper it may be, if you do not get your point across, how smart is that? Watch and learn!

"Just tell him that Jennings wants to talk to him," I replied, looking at him, reflecting his stupid gaze.

You will be happy to know that just like regular folks, Glover got switched from telephone to telephone and put on hold about ten times. The only difference was Glover was not paying for the call, and he was being paid to go around in circles.

Finally, Glover asked, "Do you want to leave a message with his secretary?"

"Yes," I replied sarcastically. "Jennings wants to talk to him!"

Glover managed to pass it on to Phiffler's secretary. He hung up the telephone and said that as I did not say what I wanted to talk about, he really could not see a man as important as the U.S. bureau chief of the U.S. marshals wanting to talk to me.

"He will call just as soon as he gets the message," I said as I stood to go.

"Well, right now he is at lunch, so you might as well go back to your job. If he calls you back it most likely won't be until tomorrow. Here, let me stamp your building pass."

I had just caught Sherlock's eye in the passageway outside our workshop when the speakers boomed out loud and garbled, "Inmate Jennings, report to case manger Glover for a legal call."

Sherlock and I shot looks and signals back and forth that said the ball was in play. I was the only other inmate he knew other than himself that could make the feds jump through hoops just to have their chain jerked.

Arriving back in Glover's office he said, "Jennings, have a seat right here and I will get him on the telephone for you." He was now displaying a reddened face. "I will leave the room if you wish after you are connected."

I just looked back at him and did not reply as I was weighting the value of him eavesdropping on my conversation.

His lethargic lifestyle along with the intake of huge amounts of large-ass food washed down with whiskey at work and beer at home had left Glover with a life expectancy of a death row inmate.

Engaging the telephone on his desk like he was in an arm wrestling contest, he was losing. He belched, opened his desk drawer, and grabbed his

Rolaids. Using his thumb in the same fashion as his cousin, the orangutan, he popped two tabs in his mouth.

"Hello, Mr. Phiffler, my name is Case Manager Glover here at Springfield, Missouri. I have an inmate....Yes....Yes, sir, I will put him....Yes, sir, I am handing him....Here, Jennings, take the phone."

"Hello, Mr. Fucking Asshole. I got the message. Now do we make a deal or do I release my tape to the street?"

"Good to hear your voice, Mr. Jennings. I hope you are in good health. How's your heart? You have not had another stress-related heart attack, I trust?"

"I can get it aired anytime I want. You know how and you know who. Then you will all look like the stupid assholes you are!"

"Well I should be able to get someone to stop by in two or three days."

"Fine, then I will expect to see your man within seventy-two hours!" I handed the telephone to Glover and walked out of the room. I could not wait to get back to my confidant and share the blow by blow.

"You know they won't wait seventy-two hours. You have to be ready now with a story so fucking infantile that only a federal agent will believe it," Sherlock interjected on the exhale of a good hit off of some Missouri silage.

"How about telling them that I got the Kryptonite," I added on the inhale of the smoke that already had me rocking back and forth as if I were at sea in a small boat. It was now time to lay down, relax my mind, and send it out to play.

*What if they arrived before you figured out what you are going to tell them, or are you just going to give up Boyce for a transfer back to a West Coast joint?*

I already know what it was they want to know. This was the information they already believed I know. So quite basically, all I will do is build my story around their expectations. Remember, I am the guy who can sell a tuna sandwich to a dolphin.

Have you ever done people watching and make up stories to go with the characters you see? I was remembering that I knew Chris as well as a friend could know someone. This means what I tell the feds will pass the test of probability by their experts.

*So you do respect the U.S. marshal as sophisticated investigators.*

Yeah, right. Before I dozed off on my bunk with a satisfied smile on my face around eight P.M., I had the premise for a wild tale. It was as perverse as the people I was going to sell it to.

It was in the wee hours of the morning when the flashlight was flashed in my face. The screw was prepared to put me in cuffs as he whispered in the dark that I had visitors. I did not know it at the time but Sherlock saw me being escorted down the hall through the big doors.

I remember feeling just a bit nervous and maybe a mite intimidated by the expected middle-of-the-night approach. Therefore I was not surprised when I saw it was the famous U.S. Marshal Larry Homminick. He was being hailed as this great man hunter! Some five thousand federal agents and almost eighteen months, and he was now here talking to me in hopes of discovering some secret, revealing information so he could stop chasing his tail.

"Well, Jennings, here you are back in prison. Now who is the stupid asshole?"

He had no more than said it when the look on his face told me he knew he would regret it. I was in the part of the institution that is off-limits for most inmates. It is where regular people are received when they come to do business with the prison, all decked out in gray carpet, gray and chrome chairs, and eggshell walls, colors you will never see on my yacht.

"I suppose that would depend on how much money you made since I last saw you, Mr. Homo-nick. I've made millions. How about you?" I cheerfully chirped at him with a grin that said I'm going to use you.

"I hear the Secret Service got the whole 12.5 million!"

"Yeah, so why did they only indict me for 7.5 million?"

"What matters, Jennings, is you are here with no money and your fate is in my hands. Either you give us what we want or I guarantee you will die right here! Not today, not tomorrow but years from now. Let me see here, your sentence ends on February 5, 1986," he said as he opened his file folder. "Therefore, I predict you will stop living on February 4, 1986.

"Look, we are not playing footsie with you any longer and Judge Thompson is not here to rescue you. Judge Waters belongs to us, we own him. Why do you think you are here and not in some nice place like Pleasanton. Your filthy-mouthed old lady lives, what, about twenty minutes from there."

I lifted my hands to gesture the fact that I was in cuffs. "If you are through saying things that will get your candy-ass kicked, you can take these cuffs off, or you came for nothing and you know that if I do not give you something tangible, Phiffler will send you to the outskirts of Juneau, Alaska, and I will make my deal with the FBI."

He instructed the screw to uncuff me and to leave the area. "You can come back in about an hour. This won't take long," Homminick said, still trying to act like he was in charge.

We bantered for about another fifteen minutes, then Homminick pulled his little recorder out of his pocket. He rewound it, erasing everything that had transpired. We sat down and one of the other two marshals that accompanied him asked if I wanted a pop or a cup of coffee.

Both Homminick and I declined and the two other marshals stepped back to the double exit doors and waited. Homminick turned the recorder back on and said, "Special Agent Homminick at 2:45 A.M. In my presence is William Brian Jennings. We are in the reception area of the Springfield, Missouri Federal Prison.

"This interview is by request of Mr. Jennings and no client-attorney issues apply for this interview. Mr. Jennings, are you here by your own will? Please identify yourself and answer the question."

"I am William Brian Jennings, and I am here without duress."

"Okay, Jennings, tell us what it is you want to tell us."

"I am prepared to answer any question that you ask about Christopher Boyce that I have knowledge of and disclose information that I have reason to believe you do not have a clue about."

"Will this information guarantee that we will be able to locate and apprehend Boyce?"

"I'm sorry, I cannot guarantee, either of those things!"

"Why not, Jennings?"

"Well it is my belief that short of tying him to a tree for you, that you do not have the ability to locate your own ass without visual aids."

Homminick clicked the tape off and backed it up.

"You erase that and we are done here and now."

Homminick played to the end of my comments and pressed record.

"Okay, Jennings, what is this new information that we do not know!"

"Not without a written commitment from Phiffler."

"Okay, Jennings, have you heard from Boyce after he went over the wall at Lompoc?"

"I have received information both directly and indirectly from Boyce after he escaped from Lompoc."

"When did you make last contact with Boyce?"

"I have not made any physical contact with Boyce after he left Lompoc!"

"You just said!"

"I know what I said. If you do not remember, play the tape back!"

"Jennings, I am not going to put up with your shit, and I am sure neither will Mr. Phiffler. Besides, we are closing in on him as we speak, as a result of his New York gun connection."

"You have been closing in on Boyce since the night he disappeared without a trace," I said, as a vision of Boyce standing on the Federal Building steps in downtown LA flashed in my head as clear as a snapshot.

*You knew Boyce had his picture taken on the steps of the Federal Building after he escaped?*

That is another one of those need-to-know things and you do not need to know. Homminick hit me with every question he could think of, which I answered in away that left him with another question. So for the last twenty minutes I was manipulating the interrogation while planting an unidentifiable idea in his head that I knew would be too tempting for him not to swallow hook, line, and sinker.

He turned the recorder off and summoned the guard to put the cuffs back on and return me to my dorm as Homminick pretended that he was not sure with what I gave him that he would be back or not.

So as we walked off in opposite directions, I threw out a careless hint. "Perhaps you should be trying to find Christina, instead of Chris!" Then the doors closed. The screw did not put me in cuffs and he only escorted me to the main tunnel and sent me on my way at 3:55 A.M.

I was dog tired when I got back to my dorm, flopping down on my bunk too exhausted to even take my shoes off. The inmates were just starting to be awakened to go to their jobs in the kitchens and the bakery.

Nothing gets done in prison that the inmates do not do. I know that the Cids have been led to believe something different. However, there is only one reason that prison works—it is because the inmates let it work. Therefore when punishment gets out of hand, the prisoners take over the prison.

When there is a prison riot do not blame the inmates; look instead to the warden and his staff. Remember, bad wardens, just like bad dictators and those who choose war, are men with the hearts of pigs and the brains of chickens. To treat with cruelty those who are in your charge or those who do not share your path just to elevate one's station in life is the proof of a volga cause formulated by a deprived mentality.

Sherlock had sold our boss on the idea that we should start cleaning the cooling towers. "Sherlock, I am dead tired. I really do not think...."

"You are going to love it, believe it," he said with a smile I had learned to trust. I have met few men in my life I call "friend," because *friend* means *defend* and that means *respect*. If you were not worthy of my respect, then you did not enter that group I call friend. For a person that has met many strangers, I have come away with too few friends.

The cooling towers were great, as was being outside and feeling the wind on my face and the unhampered sunlight streaming down on my body. We found a place where we were out of sight. As I kicked back on the boards with the sun streaming down and the sound of the water falling between the boards, reminiscent of a flume flowing into a cranberry bog, for a few moments I escaped back to the farm in Carver and let my child play down at the pond.

After respecting my private journey for as long as he could stand, Sherlock shouted at me over the sound of the falling water and my child disappeared, as my mind's holodeck shut down.

"What did you come up with? I hope you were at least as creative as I would be," Sherlock throwing out a challenge.

"You mean did I come up with an undeniable, unprovable hook of all hooks? It is still in the thinking phase but it will be based in the fabrication that

Chris is now a matronly lady, flying her falcon from some mountain, perhaps in Australia or Ireland. Oh and she may be two inches shorter than Chris."

"You got a premise for this cross-gender thing? What did you say, science fiction, not fantasy fiction?"

"Yeah, I got back-up that will fly right by a government shrink! Designed for the kind of mental health professional that would use his degree as a tool for federal law enforcement to misuse."

"What do you figure they will do next?" Sherlock asked as he drifted off on his own speculation.

"I figure they will be back in about three days with a signed transfer. They will have a clause that my story passes a lie detector test. Then Homminick will grill me for three days. He will do anything in his power to prove that my information is worthless. I will use it in my favor. I know how to push Homminick over the edge. That wimp has more twisted ideas in his head than any psycho in this joint."

"Make sure he does not use your anger for him against you!"

Homminick was back in two days with a contract. Now all I had to do was convince the U.S. marshals that Chris changed himself into a thirty-year-old tomboy about two inches shorter than he used to be and that he could be flying his bird anywhere people can fly hunting birds for sport.

I would let Homminick help me design a scenario he already believed by reading his face. All those years as a traveling salesman taught me these skills that allowed me to pitch right to the batter, because Homminick wanted a home run a lot more than he needed to get even with me.

*It's like you said before about federal agents, and it being all about how they look to the boss and how the marshals look to the Congress and the Senate from where the cash does flow.*

I still knew down deep inside that if I did not make this last grab for the safety line I would most likely die right here. Talk about inspiration—I remember one day this movie director by the name of Tom Budhal asked me if I thought I could act!

It was just two days later when Homminick and his partner had me delivered to this room in a part of the prison I had never been before. It had benches and tables dating back to the early 1900s. The room, although set up somewhat like a visiting room, had not been used in many years. Some of the visiting tables had chicken-wire frames down the middle, reminding me where I was, subtle deniable intimidation no doubt brought to me by Larry Homminick. For me it made a better stage.

It would end up taking me three days before I gave Homminick exactly what he wanted from me—the why. Why did Boyce change himself into a female?

The answer: Boyce came from a family of male pigs. Everyone Boyce was related to was an ex-high school football star now federal agent! Boyce was on the fast track to becoming his father's clone, as he was already a football star with a summer job in the TRW building, known as the Black Box, the very hub of every secret this nation had and knew about every other nation in the world.

Boyce would always leave the room whenever anyone in our clique started talking about sex in any form, and he would not become a party to any sexual talks.

All he wanted to do in life was fly his bird, and as a boyish matronly lady there would be little sexual pressure put upon him.

No, I did not think that Boyce was gay, however he did not want to become a male chauvinistic pig, as were all of his role models.

When Homminick admitted openly that he could not just believe that Boyce had turned himself into a female, I knew he had swallowed the hook.

The where: Where would he have gotten it done? My answer was either Australia or Switzerland. I still cannot believe that was not a deal breaker. However, I did cover it well with things I knew they already knew about Chris and where he could look for allies.

Where would I guess that Boyce might be now? For that, Homminick brought in a world atlas as we window shopped for those spots where I prayed to God that Boyce had not gone to. I also prayed that Chris had not really turned himself into a woman!

In the end, the Washington team of specialists who had been reviewing the daily tapes and the next day they would test what I said the day before, had finally agreed that it was time for me to be tested with the lie breaker.

*It is one thing to beat an interview, it is another to beat a lie detector. When the whole story is a lie, how does one trick the machine?*

You worry about that and I will still be worrying about how they knew that if they sent me into a maximum security prison, I would smuggle stuff into Boyce at great risk to myself. By this time I realized there was more about me that I did not know yet and that this road I am on is building itself. The only other possibility is my Destiny was more than just being the only multi-denominational counterfeiter in history. I was becoming aware of a very troubling truth about what might still be hiding in wait for me.

The next morning I was taken to the tailor shop and fitted in a well-tailored heavy gabardine suite of an ugly green and brown. Two local marshals picked me up; it was spooky to see the picture of Chris hanging from the visor. It looked just like my brother Jim did when he graduated high school. I found it amazing that the feds had not shot or arrested my brother by mistake, thinking he was Chris.

They did not take me to a nice restaurant on the way to FBI headquarters. There were still large humps of snow like they had been placed haphazardly by a city employee.

The marshal attempted to cover my handcuffs as we got out of the very generic Ford fed car, the other reason I will never own a Ford. I pushed it away and announce my indignity.

"I was only attempting to eliminate your embarrassment of being in handcuffs."

"I am Jewish. We are used to being taken into custody by government cops."

"Your records show you are a Baptist! The First Baptist Church of Carver!"

I am a genetic Jew by birthright, I was brought up in the Christian belief, however I would not share something like that with a person who was not of a group from which I sought approval!

The FBI and the U.S. marshals compete with each other for everything, including funding. I had known since Boyce went over the wire that whichever agency gets Boyce's collar gets the press and the best award from the government treasure chest.

Do not get angry with me. I did not invent this game nor was I the one who made the rules. I just played the game because if I did not play, I died. You do not keep people like me alive unless I think I owe you my soul. The only problem I had was the what I knew not what I did not know.

Going through back doors all your life, you sometimes find things you never see at the front door. Growing up in Carver, my world was very small. I rode on the neck of a Budweiser horse on the waterfront in Plymouth when I was too young to remember my age. The world looked so big up there compared to the knee-high view of a boy my age.

Now this little boy is back up on the neck of that horse and just like before, my curiosity and a quest for adventure overrode my fear.

*Curiosity and adventure, two things that have a very high death rate, I thought to remind the storyteller!*

Right now, no matter what I do, my life expectancy is about that of Mr. Glover. Some day I am going to bite off more than I can chew and choke on it. Right off the bat I saw that the FBI was going to be my best friend. They were going to be stealing my information and put their own value on it before the marshals would believe it one way or the other.

The FBI gave me a list of five questions that the marshals wrote for me to answer yes or no. "Read the questions," I was instructed. "If you cannot feel comfortable with just a yes or no answer," he told me, "then we will change the question so that you can answer honestly yes or no."

Right away Homminick jumps in, "Look, Jennings, you answer these questions yes or no or I will know you're lying!"

The FBI agent gave Homminick a look of disapproval and escorted me into the examination room. With the door closed in the fully windowed office, the FBI agent said, "What's in it for you, Jennings?"

Like the typical eight-year-old, I replied, "What do you mean?"

"Look, I know what they want and I know what Homminick wants. They did not tell us what's in it for you, Jennings!"

"You already know what I am in it for, the FBI already turned down my offer for an all expenses paid two week vacation and a transfer to Pleasanton FCI!"

"That is a co-sexual joint, isn't it?" he responded. "Relax and I will help you through this. You will pass, take my word for it."

Yeah and he probably had some low tide Florida land he would be happy to sell me. I had a better plan than hoping for help from the FBI to pull it off.

"My boss wants you to know that if he gave you the deal you wanted, he would have had to share the info with the marshals anyway. This way we get it at the same time, and we are all ready to go with it. They are not."

I am not sure but I think I was just asked to lie to the marshals and the FBI is going to help. Wow, this is so cool. It is just like Chris told me one rainy day on the twelfth floor on Front Street in San Diego. "It's a good thing that the citizens are not as immoral as the feds," Chris shared with me.

If you wait long enough, a government agent will tell you everything they know. They usually start with the stuff they are not supposed to tell you. Freely translated: They are willing to deal and they do not care if the information comes from you or they give it to you so you can give it back.

If you doubt what I am telling you, then you are one of the reasons the feds feel they have the right to lie and falsify. Some day they will lie and falsify about you or someone you love. Then it will be too late to believe—that is when reality smacks you dead in the ass.

Oh what a dangerous path you choose when you cross the path where Satan trods.

Now you know why the government has put this nation in debt. Everyone in government is fighting over our tax dollars. How many ways can you spend the money provided by just one hundred and twenty million tax-payers when all the numbers in Washington begin with a "B" or a "T"!

Was it not Kennedy who said stop asking your government to serve the people, and force the people into serving the government? I cannot be the only person who sees a conflict with our founding documents and today's leadership.

"Question number one: Do you know where Chris is now?

"No!"

"Question number two: Have you had physical contact with Boyce while you were on the street?"

"No!"

"Question number three: The information you gave to Larry Homminick regarding Boyce's activities after his escape is true and correct?

"Yes!"

"Question number four: Did Boyce contact you after his escape?"

"Yes!"

I will not disclose my method past saying that you can condition your mind to believe a lie is a truth. If you do not believe me, ask any woman. How many times have they said I did it or said it for his own good? If a woman can fake an orgasm a man should be able to fake a lie detector.

*What were you thinking at that very moment when he asked you those four questions?*

That was what I was thinking; it is my kind of yoga. I entertain myself with humor and minimize my objective. This relaxes me and gives me a false sense of well being! You know, like what you get from marijuana! *Readers Digest* has always been pro-marijuana with a whole section dedicated to the proposition "Laughter Is the best Medicine!" So you train your body to respond to internalized laughter.

The sad part for the Cids is this was the best information they had to date. Four times they gave me the test. Four times it came up that I was telling the truth and that truth was that Boyce swam out to a boat, jogged to the airfield in Solvange, or took a Greyhound to Canada on an old ticket. Four times those questions proved Boyce then went to either Australia or to Switzerland for radical surgical changes. I am sorry, Rusty, if the coincidence, coupled with your Christmas gift, brought you some problems.

*Who is Rusty and what does she have to do with Christopher Boyce and a Christmas gift?*

I should have been worried about my mother, father, and Diane as circumstances proved out. Mom and Dad were on a Greyhound from Quartzite to my brother's home in Missouri. They were somewhere in Oklahoma when three fed cars pulled the bus over and extracted my mother and father like fleeing felons. Some blamed me because our federal agents were acting like their tactics were of a different government than the one I fought for.

The reason my folks were on the bus was because they did not like the stress of flying.

They were then taken to a large hotel in Oklahoma City, where the FBI thought to interrogate my mother and father about any knowledge they had about the Falcon. They wanted to freak these two quiet-living people of goodwill toward everyone they ever encountered. The feds overlooked just one thing: My father is a firm believer in what our country was built to be, and what they were doing was no part of any of that.

I never felt real close to my dad. Hell, I was the one they were not expecting, showing up two years after my next oldest brother. Being born in 1944, things were looking kind of bleak. My dad was a serious, hard-working, well-read man with convictions of steel that he lived by, and I just had never made the connection with him until now. I had a way of always being right in front of or right behind the shit that was happening. Things have not changed; you will still find me in the front row seat of life.

My dad lit them up but good, and they put them on a federal jet, delivering them to my brother's home via limo ahead of schedule. I think that was the day my dad stopped thinking I had let him down and started realizing so had the country he served and built warships for twenty-one years.

The FBI was not done. They decided that evidence in the form of a letter could be found if they searched Diane's home. However getting a search warrant under those circumstances was not legal for good reason.

Diane reputes the idea still today that the FBI were responsible for the fire in her kitchen, which was called in within—according to the arson report—the first fifteen minutes of the fire, almost ten minutes before the nearest neighbor called it in. Although everyone got out safely and the fire was contained to the kitchen and dining room area, smoke damage was extensive. Everything had to be removed, put in storage, and de-smoked. No search warrants needed down at Federal Bekins In Storage.

However many years later, I did not find the letter taped to the inside top of the bedstand chest with the hand-carved drawer fronts or the picture of Chris standing on the steps of the Federal Building in downtown LA. It was gone but the tape marks remained. The fire could have been a coincidence, fate, or Destiny. If you have trouble believing the FBI would do anything like that, then you have not been paying attention for the last forty years.

Ten days passed before I was chained up for a federal flight. Ten days and the U.S.-less marshals had flown halfway around the world in two different directions, while the FBI shook down my family, friends, and associates. Some of them got angry with me because their government was needlessly harassing them to get even with me just in case I had tricked them in the same fashion that Chris tricked the KGB.

*"On the Road Again" must have been written just for you. Not even six months and you are moving back to California.*

I felt bad for everyone that was left behind, however one thing you try to learn in prison is you cannot do another man's time. You walk that road alone, unless you walk it with God! I know what you are thinking but you are wrong—God loves outlaws. Knowing that gave me the courage to face what lay ahead.

# CHAPTER TWELVE

*They were able* to make the trip last a whole week, with a weekend stop over in Hell, southern style, with a name to fit the ambiance, Talladega. Definition: place of short life expectancy.

Somewhere the federal government has every hate, fear, and biological abnormality of every individual American written down, just in case they ever need to use them against you. I will not be giving up any secrets if I told you that wet and dank basements give me the creeps and that oil base paints of that era gave me migraine headaches. So ending up in a dark, dank basement with freshly painted bars should not surprise anyone. Luckily the blanket, bed linens, and pillow smelled like dog farts. You know which one I had to pick.

When I stepped off the bus at Pleasanton, I had to look and smell like ten days of bad road.

"Welcome to Pleasanton, Mr. Jennings," the fat screw said, grinning ear to ear as they were inducting us in a room that had a fully glassed wall facing the inside of the prison grounds. Directly outside of the window a number of women were window shopping the newly arrived inmates. Six men and one female, and on the other side of the window the odds were three women to every man. If you took away all of the gay men and women, it still came out to three women to every man.

The prison was designed in such away as to not be aware of the fences that contained me. That also seemed to lower the tension of all the inmates. There are three dorms, two for the female inmates and one for the male inmates, with a chow hall that looked similar to a casual restaurant. The entire compound was more like a small college, complete with students studying and doing homework on the grass. This was the first institution that lived up to the name of correctional institution. The dorm rooms were singles with wood furniture and a huge, tinted picture window.

Not treating prisoners like savage animals worked well. Proof positive of the success of these institutions was Congress demanding they all be discontinued as suggested by the then-director of the Federal Bureau of Prisons,

Norman Carlson. These prisons had low disciplinary problems, almost no violence, and when released the inmates were 87 percent less likely to re-offend, the exact opposite of the rest of the prison systems both state and federal. Good cause for our leaders to hide these facts from the people who pay the bills. Still think that your side of the law is the best side to be on?

This is not heaven, however, neither is it purgatory. It is a place where an over-the-hill counterfeiter could have three girlfriends at the same time, but I was an old-fashioned kind of guy. I like to keep my girlfriends separated by at least a county line.

Co-ed prisons have to be the best idea for social re-integration of inmates back into society. All of the hate and anger in my body drained right out into the ground when my beautiful San Salvadorian girlfriend would take my hand for a stroll on the compound.

All of my life I imagined that I would be a world traveler and that one day I would marry a princess or something like that in a strange and foreign land. Now I am in a co-ed federal joint and my girlfriend is the stepdaughter of the ex-vice president of El Salvador. She was as close to a princess as I would ever see; she wore three different outfits every day. She always had everything in perfect order and although she spoke no English and I spoke no Spanish, we could spend hours together. We were never at a loss for words. Somehow, I always knew when she would tell me that she loved me and when she wanted me to kiss her. I would run like a puppy dog to catch up when she would tug at my hand and say "Bent`a bent`a!" She would look back at me with a smile that ate up her whole face.

*You cheated on Diane after only being down for less than a year and being transferred to that prison just to be near her?*

Diane and I did not put those restrictions on each other. We knew better than to make rules and promises that served to promote jealousies. Besides, I did not want to be with a woman that had denied herself sex for six years. That would have to redefine the meaning of bitch.

Diane knew about my girlfriend and I knew about her boyfriend. I was in prison, opportunity knocked, and I jumped on it. My time with Edith is best remembered as a rustling fire burning on a beach under a bright night sky on the Pacific Coast of the Yucatan Peninsula. For a time I realized my childhood fantasy of falling in love with a princess. However it was not perfect and would not last.

It was the summer of 1981 and I was back in California. Life was sweet and hydraulic engineering was my specialty. So my boss put me in charge of getting the automatic sprinkler system operating correctly and create drainage that the government designers got wrong. This gave me access to the blueprints outside the fence and the employee and visitor parking area. I also worked in areas inside the fence that were off limits to everyone but me and the one who cut the grass.

It was not long before I had an income from my pipeline of drugs with accessories. So I never had to get in line at the commissary for any of my other needs. Diane visited regularly and saw to it that I had clothes to match my comfort style. From my western-cut three-piece suit to my black hat, boots, jeans, and track shoes, I was stylin' prison style, learning once again that just when you start singing, zippied do-da, the sidewalk is about to make contact with your ass.

It was one of those nice sunny days with nothing to do but get high and enjoy the sunshine. It's free in prison.

"Jennings," rang out from my destiny. Peter Avillinoza, my case manager was paging me.

I turned around to see the man Will Rogers would not have liked if he met him.

"Jennings, come in here a minute. We need to talk about your upcoming parole hearing."

"You have me on the list. That's all I have to know."

"Well I need to know more, so either conference with me or I will cancel you for this go around."

"Fine," I said as I stepped into his office and took a comfortable chair so I could look out the window.

Avillinoza tucked his tie into his cocoa-colored suit as he seated himself behind the desk with the cheap plastic nameplate. "What do you want, Jennings?"

"You called me out. What do you want?"

"No, no, Jennings, what do you want from the parole board. You know, what would you like them to give you?"

"You mean besides the regular blowjob? Well, how about a two-year date with a six-month halfway house. That would put me on the street in about six months from the hearing date."

"I know you are joking, Jennings, but I'm not. I could make that happen!"

I turned to look at him. Up until just then I had been gazing out the window at some young camp cuties.

He was tapping his finger on the page in my file that stated that I went out on a fifty thousand dollar cash surety bond. It was obvious. The twinkle in his eyes told me that he knew what all of that meant.

"You're a real special case, Jennings," he said, holding his finger on the word cash. "You just give me the word and you will be in a halfway house twenty minutes from your old lady."

"I would have to see if I could afford a break like that," I said as I stood to leave. As my hand grasped the doorknob I turned my head to look into his eyes so there would be no mistake. "I will make a phone call and get back to you on Monday for where and when."

I left the office and did not look back. I already knew that it was done from my end. I just needed Avillinoza checked out, to make sure that he was fronting for someone at regional headquarters or higher.

Sunday afternoon I spoke directly to Zuba about Avillinoza.

Zuba's reply was, "We have done business with him before. He knows the routine. Just tell him that I am handling it. He knows who to call! Do not call again until you are on the street, oh and I own your ass!"

For some reason, I felt nothing special was about to happen in regards to my release from prison. Edith was also being played in a way not consistent with others charged with the same crime. Like myself, her problems seemed to be greater than just being in prison because she broke the law. Therefore, I decided to check out her pre-parole report. You see I am dyslexic, left-handed, and a lithographer by trade, which means I can read upside down. All I need is Edith's counselor to open it up and thumb through it for me.

As it happened her pre-parole hearing interview was scheduled on a Saturday afternoon. Edith's counselor liked me, as did most of the staff at Pleasanton FCI. They thought that Edith and I made a real cute couple. With my full, bristly, gray-black beard, Edith was the cute part and I was the couple part. She was eager for me to go and listen to what her counselor had prepared for her presentation.

The staff's personnel involvement in the inmate's parole hearing is not consistent with the rest of the federal prison system. Which is all irrelevant now that there is no more parole in America's federal prison system, putting the U.S. in the group of dictatorship and third world nations, a fatal mistake of the lawmakers, along with the three strikes and you're out law! Both void of all and any logic, therefore they are constitutionally incorrect.

*What is illogical about life sentences for repeat offenders?*

Do you still live by the same clichés as when you were eighteen to twenty-one? Do you still hold the same beliefs and understanding for life that you had when you were thirty-something? If you answered yes to one or both, then you are right—you should be imprisoned for stupidity for life. However most humans tire of swimming against the current. By the time you reach the forty to fifty zone, you think differently, and things you thought you could not live without no longer interest you at all. No, I do not mean sex!

The law denies maturity in a land where all cops and judges become corrupt while still in service, and outlaws become honest, productive citizens while serving time. To not believe that is a contradiction of human kind.

Two Bushes, the same bad fruit! By the time my grandchildren accept the burden of the Bush war on the world, 75 percent of the prison system will be doing life and over fifty. That will cost an average of more than one hundred thousand dollars a year per inmate, the equivalent of more than twenty law abiding citizens on Social Security.

The government can afford the worst prison system in the world, but they cannot stop stealing one hundred and sixty-three million dollars a day from the Social Security income. They call it a short fall, like they called killing a man in the dentist chair an inmate overdose.

Before you let the government convince you that all Americans are bad and will never be good, think back to when you wet the bed—did you never stop or did you grow out of it? The government is never going to get better as long as you believe in their opinion of you. Our mistakes and shortcomings are held up by our leadership government as a good cause for more repressive laws while the fraud, deceptions, and squandering of trillions of our hard earned and sacrificed tax dollars are lost in the false barrages of finger pointing by both the dumercrates and the republicant's, the ones that have collectively agreed to never admit the truth!

*I know by now that all of this must be relevant to both you and Edith! So I will just wait and see why this is all relevant.*

It worked out just like I had choreographed the whole thing. Edith, all decked out in her spring tennis outfit, was seated in the chair dead in front of the desk. I stood behind Edith with my hands on the back of the chair, giving me a bird's eye view of the folder on Ms. Davenport's desk.

*How could you disseminate all of the information in an inmate's file from that distance when someone else was turning the pages?*

Federal prison employees are selected based on how close they score to a seventh grade mentality, and the ones who got straight A's in grammar school, junior high, and high school. The ones who think that doing something right is the same as doing what they are told. That is why the government grades the employees in the same fashion as they were graded in school.

Everything in the file is labeled with different colored tabs. Some pages or sections could have several different colored tabs. Therefore the colored tabs correlate to the section or page titles they are displayed on indicate just what shelf the government put you on. More color's more trouble; the silent beef is denoted with the same three colors over and over again.

I swear if I had known what I learned just two years later down the road, I would have not done what I thought I had to do after Edith's parole board hearing. She was torn with wanting to go home to her life and her children and wanting to be very close to me. Edith cried as she dragged me to her counselor's office so she could make me understand.

Ms. Davenport did not understand why the parole board denied Edith her earliest chance to go home. She was not a criminal; she was a humanitarian doing what the government failed to do on purpose.

"Mr. Jennings, it is my understanding that if she breaks up with you, they will respond to her national appeal, and she could go home soon."

It did not matter whether I understood it or not, I would make Edith break up with me. I knew how to trigger her genetic anger. I started having people pay me off in the chow hall during commissary days. Edith automatically assumed I was dealing drugs, and drugs were something Edith did not tolerate. She was like a roman candle lit off in the chow hall. She was reading me up one side and down the other in Spanish. She did not know it but she was buying her ticket home and she convinced everyone that she was breaking up with me for good.

Peter Avillinoza disappeared and I was assigned a new case manager. I, of course, got no play from the parole board. It was not surprising that the marshals would still be waiting on a chance that I would falter. What I did not expect was to be screwed with by the Secret Service.

My new unit manager was the in house, federal agent wannabe. Fred would remind me everyday that the feds were closing in on Boyce. What totally cracked me up was the day he told me they had him cornered in South Africa. It was that same week when he summoned me to his office to receive a call from the U.S. Secret Service. I had already figured out Avillinoza was jerked out of this joint because he was selling what was not up for sale—me.

The phone rang and Fred just told me to pick it up. "Hello, Jennings." He told me his name but I have no recollection what it was. "I just want you to tell me what you know about two hundred and sixty thousand dollars of your counterfeit that just hit the street in Chicago last week."

"I would like to help you out but I've been in lock-up for the last nine months. Why don't you ask the rats you gave the street to."

"Look, Jennings, you give me any shit and I will beef you all over again in Chicago and get you the bitch in Illinois. You know what joint that puts you in!"

"You go do that, Mr. Fuck Head, and I will tell a judge and a jury everything I know about how that money got on the street and I will walk on both beefs. In other words, go suck your mother's cock."

"Jennings!" he screamed, out of control as I slammed the receiver down so hard it broke in two.

Fred never said another word to me and I was soon to end up on the short list for transfer. As it turned out, they sent me down the road via Terminal Island to a place called Boron Federal Prison Camp.

# CHAPTER THIRTEEN

***Boron looked like*** a set from the *Twilight Zone*. The town resembled a dried-up cow chip, located adjacent to the Edwards Air Base, home of the shuttle-craft and the taxi plane.

I know what you are thinking, and this time you are right. It is no accident that the government planted me here. Neither was it an accident that in addition to working heavy equipment, I took a base job. Once every day an inmate would drive a bus load of inmates to the highly secure air base.

Oh, it gets better than that! Of all of the manual task jobs I could have been assigned to, the one they chose was the paper recycle detail. I was assigned to a sergeant who would drive me to every high security area on the base and I would gather up all of the used printouts and punch cards. Then we would go back to the warehouse where I would unload it onto pallets and strap them down with steel binders. That and breakfast, coffee breaks, and sight seeing tours to the sergeant's regular assignment station made up the day.

Sometimes they would assign a female sergeant, and sometimes that added additional stops to the daily run, but mostly I preferred homemade chocolate cake! I had reached the age that sex just for sex was not what I wanted any longer. It only took forty years.

One to two days a week I was left just wandering around on my own all day. Everything was so easy; I had an ID card that had a big red "P" on the back.

With my special "P" for privilege pass I walked up and touched the shuttle *Columbia*, stood under the open boom doors of the B-1 bomber, and sat in the cockpit of an F-111 fighter. I even saw the Stealth when it was still a secret.

One day this inmate from the Berkley Vietnam war protest days pointed out a design abnormality about the entire facility. I checked it out from the hilltop rocket site for myself and found a reality of truth that caused me to change my mind and go back to driving my John Deere tractor. I got to see the shuttle landing from the hilltop at the prison camp as I filled my days grading roads and building waste water ponds.

I had more freedom at camp. It was not just a rumor that when the camp warden wanted to drive his warden car he had to get the keys from me. I did have errands to run and it was two miles to the nearest liquor store. I would drive the car to town to pick up parts for the repair shop and stop by and pick up the phoned-in liquor order. Then I would drop it off out on the highway, where I would retrieve it later that day with my John Deere tractor or runners would go out at night and bring it in.

*Wouldn't the liquor store clerk know you are a prisoner? You did say this was a one cow flap town?*

Why would he want to know, so he could lose four to eight hundred dollars a week in non-reportable income? All he had to do was tally up a ticket, put the bottles in boxes, and beer by the case, and receive an envelope with exactly the right amount plus a tip. It was where they got the idea years later.

*What idea? Who?*

The idea *don't ask don't tell*! What you think Clinton came up with that? He was the only one that told the truth about using marijuana. Yeah, like Ronnie brought down the wall with a single sentence. Hello; the television inspired the people and the people brought the wall down. *Hogan's Heroes* set the standards for federal prisoners.

*Why did you really quit your base job?*

Opportunity, too many opportunities. Back door opportunities that could result in big bucks. Too many temptations to roll government dollars into my pocket. The risk level was high on the fluke scale. More federal outlaws get busted by the fluke factor than for any other reason. Besides I was being manipulated by the feds, and they owned the key. You might say I got weary of committing crime that the government profited from and I didn't. They wanted me to escape, you know, in a big way and it would have been just too easy.

Diane came by to visit me after a garment industry show in LA, a buying trip for her store. It was a long way off the beaten track, but she would keep her promise to me because that's who she was. The flame was still flickering, however Diane felt that if I stopped kicking the feds in the nuts I would be closer and closer to coming home.

*Why didn't you just escape? You still had reason to believe that they intended to kill you at the very end of your sentence.*

It was me versus the feds and you just do not walk away from a challenge like that, if you are me. If I ran, the story my children would be told would just be too devastating. I would rather die in prison than to have the feds tell my kids I ran to be free, when if I loved them I would have stayed and done my time, like a man.

I knew I would one day figure it all out. I needed to stay in the game long enough to find the answers I was looking for—the WHY! I was not without some ideas; I just did not like that picture so I spent a long time trying to find the wrong answers. The reality did not sink in for many years to come but when it did, it flooded my mind with the blatantly obvious.

Destiny would prove that Boron was put on my agenda for me to meet people who would broaden my knowledge base. This place was not working well for the feds. They had put me there in hopes that I would escape and kill Bogart as he had used himself up as a rat. So they pissed me off and I went off on my chronic alcoholic case manager. He got scared and after only eight months I was U.S. marshal-bound for Terminal Island Federal Prison for re-designation to prison number four.

# CHAPTER FOURTEEN
## WHERE THEY ALL COME TOGETHER

*I wasn't out* on the yard two minutes when someone called out my name loud enough for the Coast Guard to hear. I popped my head up to the bright Southern California sunshine and saw one old friend from my last stay. Everyone that did not know me knew for sure I was not a rat or I would have shrunk from view at the sound of my name. Crazy Bobby with his tattooed back that proclaimed "San Diego" was my welcome announcement. He said, "It's old home day for sure now, Jennings. You are going to like it here, man."

As soon as I started down the walk known as "the Freeway" to the south yard, someone reached out and pulled me into a well-shadowed corner and stuck a joint in my lip. Moving on, I was neck-hooked by Big John, the guy I almost nut shot just two years ago, and again they forced good herb on me. By the time I reached the south yard I was so high I forgot why I had come. So I watched the sun burn red-hot into the sea and reminisced about Edith, Diane, and my children that I had not seen or heard from in years. My ex-wife told me they did not want to hear from me ever again unless I sent her one thousand dollars a month. That was doable. Except she demanded a five hundred dollar advance to call collect. She received the five hundred dollars then refused my calls. I knew if I sent her one thousand dollars a month she would not make them available for visits.

I possessed one thing she did not understand; I have the patience of Job. My children would grow up and in time they would understand that life does not make guarantees. Shit happens to everyone regardless of how right or wrong they might be living their lives. The only thing you guarantee your children is to love them. More than that is just a chance on a highway full of drunk drivers. I'll be there for the long run and I will know and love their children as well. In the words of Forrest Gump, that's all I'm going to say about that!

I hooked up quick to the T.I. pipeline and found out the marshals had me scheduled for a trip to Tucson, Arizona. Without giving up any secrets the computer automatically bumped me off the ship list for four months while I visited with old friends from both the street and the joint.

It did not last forever and once again, I was air bound to Tucson by Evergreen Air, the official airline of the Federal Bureau of Prisons. Evergreen referred to the age and experience of the pilots that flew the government slave ships with men chained hand to foot at fifteen thousand feet. The pilots were so young they looked like they just went from flying kites to jets.

Tucson was open only a year when I arrived; my new counselor greeted me with, "Where in hell have you been, Jennings? We have been expecting you for the last four months!"

"I'm sorry," was my reply. "I needed a little time off from my hectic prison schedule, me time."

The big surprise was my new unit case manager was none other than the very disgruntled Peter Avillinoza. It was almost Christmas time so he left me with his best Christmas wishes.

"I will be back in two weeks, Jennings, and you will be out on that compound raking rocks, eight and five every week for the next five years. You got that, Jennings; I am going to make your life a living hell. Your spotless record will read so bad that the parole board will never give you a date."

His face was so red I feared he might drop dead right on the spot, and they would beef me for it.

"Well, Peter, the way I see it, I'm the reason you are here, you are not the reason I am here. So you better change your shit or I will see you doing time before I finish all of my time."

Then he kicked me out of his office while a dorm full of inmates watched in disbelief. I just shrugged my shoulders and said, "It's a gift. I just have a way with the federal subculture."

I swear to the good Lord up above that I had no idea nor did I have a clue that I would actually make it happen. Then two months later I met Satan. I had seen him around the compound a few times. He may not have been Satan, but he was blood relation. His name was Angel, an ex-semipro boxer who barged about beating people to death while high on PCP.

He killed a prison guard at San Diego MCC and was a revered soldier of the Mexican Mafia. Just looking him in the eye made my blood run cold with an unnatural fear.

It took a few months before I realized that Avillinoza had personally commissioned Angel to take me out. I was leaving E dorm late one noon hour and as I slipped past Avillinoza's office, I heard Angel engaged in a conversation that was going to cost all of my credibility to prove and almost cost me my life.

Unluckily I knew the major player being set up for Peter to take down or I swear I would have just shut up and watched it go down.

*Yeah, right!*

Well that and the fact Bobby was my only source for anti-tension medicine my heart needed. Not the nitroglycerin the feds issued based on my heart history provided to them by the U.S. Navy.

I got to Bobby's room in F dorm just before the after-work count. I told him so much about what was going to happen that night he had no doubt I was on the square, that coupled with the fact that he also never liked Angel.

"So when Angel comes for his kick down, what are you gonna do?" I asked when I realized it was too late to stop the delivery cycle.

The bust was scheduled for after it was cut up, so Angel could get his cut, which was the signal for the takedown to begin. This would make Avillinoza look good and maybe they would forgive him for what he had done.

*What had he done?*

He tried to sell early release to a person who was down for other reasons.

"Me," Bobby said. "I'm just going to tell him he ain't getting his cut."

That's not how it went down. I had smoked a joint with Harold then we backed it up with one of those cigars with the wood tip. We started playing spades in the common area. Visiting was over and the activity had an anticipation that something big was going down.

Angel arrived on schedule for his kick down. "You don't get any kick down, Angel," Bobby demanded.

"Why not?" Angel asked, already out of control with the need he could not control.

"Because you are a rat, Avillinoza's rat," Bobby returned as if the word "rat" was a curse word.

"Who said so?"

"Jennings said so. He heard you and Peter Avillinoza setting the whole thing up!"

While that was happening I was just getting ready to go to bed. The walking cop received a radio call and went off to the other wing of the dorm. Then Angel came through the double doors with so much force they nearly came off the hinges.

"Jennings!" he called out loud and clear as the inmates lined up on the rails of the upper tier. "This time you have gone too far! Take it back, Jennings, or I will kill you right here and now."

Too stupid to run, I kicked back in my chair and calmly said, "Settle down, Angel, it won't do any good for me to take it back," I replied with his bent up arm and knuckled up fist inches from my head.

"Why not, Jennings?"

"If I took it back you would still be a rat!"

The next thing I knew I was hit with a cannon ball and went rolling head over heels slamming my head into the concrete floor more than once. If I had not been totally stoned and relaxed, I would have died right then and there. Then Angel jumped on my chest and commenced bouncing my head off the floor several times as I visualized a watermelon being dropped out of the back of a pick-up truck onto a paved road. Harold was the only one that jumped in and pounced on Angels' back.

Angel stood up and shrugged Harold off while looking up into the faces of two hundred and fifty inmates, turned, and stormed off. Harold helped me up and back to my room as everyone disappeared or went back to what they were doing. No one but the rats saw anything. No one but the rats would report it to the staff. Now I was being tested. Would I hold my mud or PC to the hole and give up Angel?

I had some other concerns at the moment. I realized I had a concussion with a quick evaluation of my life signs. That would have been fine except no sooner had I laid down on my bunk than I started to jerk around in kind of a frightening way.

I grabbed Harold by the arm because he was freaking and that was my job. "Go get the Hack. Tell him I had another angina attack and that I fell down the stairs to the lower tier."

He started to go and I grabbed him back. "Make sure everyone knows that I need medical attention and that's all it's about."

The staff carried out my request even though they knew the true story, but if I did not say it then their hands were tied. They needed me to get a rat jacket, and then they could off me anytime they wanted. That, however, was the feds' plan.

After forty-five days in the hole, I thought I had recovered pretty well. If I refused the yard for ninety days they must ship me. I did not have to tell them why I was refusing the yard.

However, the Mexicans, Indians, and Italians wanted me to take the yard. That's all I knew the day I went back to "Main Line."

They sent me to F dorm. It was bright outside on the main compound. Every eye was on me as I walked across the barren ground. The dorm cop waited for me at the door. She was a not too unattractive woman with black hair and a deep ingrained smile on her almost demure face, void of make-up. If she had just tried a little, she would have been too attractive to do her job effectively. As it was the inmates worshipped her and went out of their way to make sure every watch she stood was a good one.

She escorted me up to the second tier. The upper landing was crowded; I had no idea so many Mexicans were in F dorm. The doorway to the two-man room was packed as Evelyn shooed them away. In the room was this huge Indian with a well pock-marked face that was sporting some other scars that did not come from jerking off or greasy potato chips.

I was followed into the room by the main man. He snapped his fingers and the door was closed and blocked from the outside by two large boys. In traditional language of the time and culture, the main man grinned at me and instructed me on what was going down. He told me to go out on the yard after count. "Jennings, go anywhere you want, talk to anyone you want. If Angel makes one move on you he will be dead before he gets within ten feet. Just look around and you will see over two hundred men got your back.

"My old lady would have been busted if you had not put the point on Angel. You got you some kind of balls, man. Hector here is your road dog. He will be with you twenty-four and seven. Stay on the yard, Jennings, so we can humiliate Angel and then they will ship him. We will kill him at his new prison as soon as he steps off the bus."

I still did not have my moxie back yet but I was up for walking around in a space bigger then eight by nine.

Hector saw I did not want the top bunk so he quickly remade both bunks while apologizing for getting it wrong. Then he provided chocolate milk and cookies and my spirits began to rise. Then a young little homeboy jumped through the door talking faster than my ears could comprehend and dropped a bulging joint into Hector's enormous hand and as suddenly as he appeared, he was gone.

"You are wanted on the yard. Do you want to smoke this now or after we get back?"

"Let's take a couple of quick hits and hit the bricks. We will finish it up when we get back from the stroll."

What happened next has been in every prison flick you have ever seen. Even though nothing happens, the director uses the camera for effect. At first I did not see Angel. Harold walked out of E dorm and joined me in the middle of the compound. The air was warm and thick but the tension in the air cracked through it like thunder. Every eye was on me and every time my eyes met up with Hispanic eyes I would get a smile and thumbs up. Everyone wanted to be the "Barto" who brought Angel to the ground. That, however, was not the plan. To kill a soldier of the Mexican Mafia before it was approved by a higher authority was not acceptable.

Harold and I talked for some time. "Bill," he said, "that cop you think set you up, he didn't. The captain set you up. I mean other than Bobby fronting you out like that was not cool. Anyway, that cop you call slow talkin' Sam, he called me into the records office and left Angel's file out on the desk while he went to go eat his supper. Seems that Angel is wired all the way to Washington via the DEA. He gets a paycheck every month. When they put him in the hole, he goes home to his old lady's home in San Pedro. She runs the bar the feds gave him after he killed the prison guard in San Diego. Do you need to know more?"

"No, but I been hanging paper on Avillinoza for forty-five days. Have you heard anything?"

"You bet. He has been arrested, Federal, but they got him stashed in an Arizona state joint PC'd. Everywhere he goes the Mexicans try to kill him. You started some shit, Bill."

"You need any smoke, Harold? I got a guy holding a half a joint."

"Are you kidding? The day you went to the hole the Mexicans threw cover all over me. It was cool; Angel started coming at me making noise like when he came down on you. Then swoop, fifty Mexicans dropped in and Angel backed off. He went in the hole but that night he flew back to San Pedro."

"Ever since then somebody drops a joint on me every night without fail. It's not often someone crosses social boundaries to watch another man's back. The Chicanos were blown away by what you did. It was real stand up, Bill, and really stupid," he closed with a grin.

"What about what you did, Harold? You were the only one that jumped in. If you had not done that just then I'd be a dead man. I owe you."

I was getting quite tired. It had turned out that I had a severe concussion. As I had not been hospitalized, I was not rehabilitating as fast as I should.

*Why did they not take you to a hospital? You were not listed as a flight risk.*

They were hoping against hope that I would die from a blood clot or a brain aneurysm. They did not want a real hospital to contradict the manufactured medical records created by the United States Navy and the Federal Bureau of Prisons.

I would have to be paranoid to explain any of what I have learned so far. Somebody wanted me to help Christopher Boyce escape. I could not have done it without the aid of a lot of people. The CIA, a Mafia Family, and somebody who knew me well enough to know I would do it without question. Somebody recorded every move on film.

They have been using my money like it was mad money. So what in hell did I do that did not serve their needs better than mine? Shit just don't add up, and I'm stuck back at WHY? So the game ain't over yet!

What in hell did Edith have to do with it? I recalled that a week before the parole board hearing at Pleasanton, her counselor casually said that I should break up with Edith just for her sake.

*It will have to end like a cheap mystery. They will have you tied up and the fuse lit to the dynamite and some tub of shit in a cheap suit would say, "Well, Jennings, the reason all this shit happened is because—well, too late now, the fuse is too short. Tell ya later!"*

Each place I went I met people, special people that on any other path I would have never known existed. More significantly was that these same people would show up over and over again.

115

As nice as the yard was, it was not nice enough for me to stay. If I do ninety days in the air conditioned hole they have to ship me and I did not want to stay in this hot, dirty, piece of purgatory in addition to doing time. I explained everything to Jose and Hector, not wanting to disrespect everything they were willing to do for me. I told them I had to do my own time on my terms.

Then I returned to the hole on Monday. Eighty-nine days, eighty-nine, thousand sitting back pull-ups on my bunk, eighty-nine thousand push-ups and squats, to the minute they rolled me up and shipped me back to TI.

A little more than two and a half years just disappeared into six transfers to five different federal prisons. Not a record, but not the norm either.

You see, when an inmate is transferred too many times, it could mean he is a rat. Just the speculation of that could get you killed. Yes, if you are counting that was attempted murder by proxy, number three, or paranoia laced with coincidence number six.

Boyce had been captured, sent back to prison. Lindsay's second book *Flight of the Falcon* was on the shelf and I was back in TI. I knew in my gut that I was not going to move again. Moving me had not worked, plus from now on everyone I had met would come to see me at TI. WHY? I did not yet have any answers, but I sensed they were coming, that or more questions.

TI housed the who's who of the federal prison west coast institutions. I was someone who stood out, for at that time in my life I resembled the Hulk; you know, the green guy, but I had a real full beard, long hair by then, and I was not green. I could not understand why people stepped wide around me until I took a serious look in the mirror. I scared myself. I got a haircut and trimmed my beard. My eyes are a milky gray when I'm in prison and crystal blue when I'm free and in love. Whether you knew me or not I looked quite dangerous. At least I looked human when Diane came to visit on her buying trip to LA's garment district.

I was given a new prison name, "Killer." I took second place in the middle weight-lifting competition, losing to the man labeled "the peddler." I needed to get a job that I could turn into a business. Being a salad chef in prison was not a big heart into it job for me. I needed more, so I stopped the prison administrator in the corridor.

"I'm your new printer," I said, verbally poking him in the chest.

"I already have a printer," he returned with an elevated authority.

"The printer you have is an Eastern Airline pilot and a Cuban from Castro's own air force."

"What are your qualifications? Excuse me, I did not get your name?"

"I'm Jennings and I printed more than fifteen million dollars worth of twenties, fifties, and hundreds."

"You got the job. I will tell Penta after he gets back from lunch!"

"No need," I replied. "I already discussed the matter Penta, and he is anxious to get back to painting murals."

"Fine, Jennings, tell him to start painting the mural in education tomorrow and one more thing, Jennings—next time ask first, if it's not too much trouble."

"Yes, sir, I surely will and Penta has already started on the corridor wall outside education," I said as the administrator mumbled at himself going down the hallway.

We have found that the prison system runs a whole lot better when we handle things among ourselves. If we had let this job transfer go through proper channels it would have taken a week and generated at least fifty hours of work and fifty pounds of paper.

The older staff members do almost nothing, which is what they are best qualified for, and let their inmate clerks do all the work, which is what they are best qualified to do.

As thanks for getting him out of the print shop, Penta painted a very large and very fine portrait of me in fifteenth century period clothes. The whereabouts of that portrait elude me like the picture of the truth that I cannot make materialize in my mind.

It is always good to see your old friends, but prison is not the place to say how good it is to see you. Tramp got busted on a five-year-old fluke. It seems back several years ago, Tramp was short a few grand on a deal, his car overheated, and he had left it at the curb. He took his gun out of the glove box and walked into a bank and held up the teller for exactly the amount he needed, winked at the teller, and left.

Years later the bank teller was on her way home when her car overheated and she stopped into a club to wait for the sun to go down. Tramp came in, sauntered up to the bar, and started hitting on her with the line, "I think I know you from somewhere." She played him, excused herself to call her girlfriend. She called the cops and went back to join Tramp until the cops came and arrested him. Tramp cannot figure out why she won't come and visit him so they can date later. If you knew Tramp, you knew he is sincere when he would say, "I wish I knew why she won't call me back."

Richard S. arrived from Tucson, David was there from Boron, and Crazy Bobby was back from San Diego on an old string of bank jobs. Every week more people from my past arrived. Over a dozen from Tucson, and one of them a deeply buried Mexican rat. I never liked him or trusted him in Tucson. It had nothing to do with his disfigured eye and his sloppy, overweight, out-of-shape appearance. He always appeared to be listening and watching more than what is appropriate for prison.

I was still filing a writ to vacate my sentence, as I did not commit the crime they convicted of committing.

*Oh, come on now—are you claiming that you did not print the money?*

Not on your life. When you do what I did you want to have it correctly recorded and charged. We have our own record books; we want it to be correct.

They had known all of the relevant information, so why did they alter everything including the error that first tipped me off? The leased 1979 Cougar XR7 was listed and reported as a *1978* Cougar XR7! Not important, you may say, however it stacked up pretty good in the WHY column. That started me looking at the entire investigation report and I realized everything was just a shade off from the truth.

The "Why" to that was easy and the reason I knew "Why" the government does that to some of us. You can never prove you did not do something that never happened unless you use a tactic they did not think of but I did. You just tell a better lie, trump that! They have to admit the truth to prove you are lying. That is why my writ was going all the way through the process and ordered back to Judge Waters to vacate my sentence.

It is not often that an inmate wins the Circuit Court, but this was TI. I was halfway done with the six and the local university was using a grant to provide legal assistance to prisoners for administrative and parole board issues only. The grant disallowed assistance for wrongly incarcerated or oversentenced inmates.

However they were lawyers and the inmates are conmen and manipulators, so we found a way around that rule. I was coming out of the hole for the second time since arriving at TI. The first word I got was that Big Mac was down on a violation. A quick check of the time told me where I would find Big Mac. When I reached the Freeway to the south yard that ran down the edge of Los Angles Harbor, there at the other end coming toward me was the six-foot-seven, 315-pound, self-made godfather, Big Mac. I made some animal attack growls and rushed toward him like I was going to run him down. It was not until I jumped right on him that he finally realized who this 169-pound, five-foot eight-inch, bearded fool was. The best part was the look on the faces of the entourage that followed along with Big Mac after his midday workout.

They did not know what to do with the little guy who was totally whaling on this giant of a man who nearly killed a cop by just backhanding him. The fact was that was why Mac was here and of course, I would be the one who came up with the gimmick that his lawyers so skillfully pulled off involving a lie detector test that the cop failed.

Tramp got shipped, kicking and screaming, to a prison camp. A man I had first met at Camp Lompoc on my first beef replaced him. This is one of those places in my story that requires a made up name. He was the Lompoc Camp barber when I first learned his name, but I always referred to him as "Half Fast." I remember I did not like him much then. He seemed to talk down to me anytime I had a conversation with him. I was told he was a gun dealer. That would be like saying I was a forger. Shawn was much bigger in the arms business than I could possibly imagine. I did not understand why Shawn was now going out of his way to befriend me this time.

This time he treated me with a good deal of respect. Over the next few weeks I slowly was exposed to the reason Half Fast was at TI. He was taken off a flight that was grounded in Miami out of Colombia for a bogus nose wheel problem. Then the feds flew him three thousand miles before they put him in prison.

I had thought that he had been busted because he bailed on an appeal trial release bond. However, that had nothing to do with it at all. Half Fast was being held for ransom by our ex-CIA chief. It seemed that there was this skinny jarhead who was forcing Half Fast to provide enough weapons to wage a fair-sized war.

It was a warm Sunday afternoon and Half Fast had indicated that he wanted to have a one on one with me. We were seated in the bleachers overlooking the view of the Queen Mary. I remember challenging him about being forced to do the single largest deal he had done since the sixties.

His reply was almost resentful. "You don't know what they are doing down there, Bill," referring to countries of Central America.

It sounded like Boyce all over again when he had said to me several years earlier, "You do not know what they are really doing, Bill."

I was just beginning to understand the things that the international crime families had long since accepted about the moral ethics of our government. We had become our own enemy. Half Fast went on to relay what I had no doubt was firsthand knowledge. All the time that Reagan was proclaiming that we were not doing business with terrorists, we were doing some of the biggest business ever with terrorists.

In many cases we were the terrorists, sometimes killing our own CIA agents dressed like priests to demonstrate how ruthless this enemy government leadership had become. Later they would tell the loved ones of those murdered agents that they died in action at the hands of some evil drug family.

He continued for more than an hour, relaying information that seemed decades and worlds away from where I thought I was viewing these events from. Before we parted I was thinking about going and smoking a joint to rid my mind of information that I really did not think I needed to remember.

"All I can say, Shawn, is I'm glad I'm not involved in any of this."

Then Shawn did something that men did not do in normal contact between two Caucasians of our persuasion. He gripped my knee sincerely, looked me dead in the eyes, and said, "You are, Bill, you are involved just like me."

When you live in a place where you can get shanked by mistake at any time, day or night, you become callous about the danger that surrounds you. What Shawn had implied did not seem to be much of a threat on the bigger scale of surrounding events.

As it happened I was sneaking away from work early so I could take a shower while the showers were still clean. I made my way from the shrink's office down the shady side of the building to the security door that led upstairs to B dorm. My timing was impeccable as Fat Smith, the black screw assigned to B dorm, exited the door. As he waddled his way across the north compound toward control, I slipped up and grabbed the handle as it hung there waiting to close that last inch. I crept up the steel and concrete stairs and peered through the doorway at an angle at the glass walls of the offices of B dorm.

Shawn was seated at the desk in the head case manager's office and there was not one staff member in sight. There were three phones on the desk that had not been there before. Seated in a chair next to Shawn was his bookkeeper with his laptop computer also plugged into the FTS lines. In front of Shawn on the desk were his albums of wartime weaponry, including fighter aircraft and long and short range missiles with assorted warheads. Standing at parade rest with their backs to the glass wall were three feds. They looked and acted like typical CIA.

Just at the moment the phone rang, Shawn looked up and saw me peering through the doorway. We made eye contact and Shawn picked up the phone and nodded his head with his hand held up like a traffic cop. Then he beckoned the feds to come forward as he drove his finger down repeatedly on the picture in his album. As the feds stepped forward in perfect unison and looked down at Shawn's finger, I moved quickly, smoothly, and without sound to the entry hall on the other side of the common area.

By this time, I was not surprised to find this side of the dorm void of any inmates. The back door was knocking and I had to go peek at the absurdity that was going on just a heartbeat away. However my heart was not beating, as I had it clutched tightly in my teeth.

Did you ever wonder what it would feel like to be present at the very moment the Constitution was signed, when Lincoln went to the theater for the last time, or when Martin Luther King took his final step? I did not know what they would call the event that I was only one of seven who knew where and how it really happened. I knew destiny just bit me in the ass again.

*So now you knew why the staff and the parole board wanted you and Edith broken up.*

Not exactly. You see, I did not understand what Shawn was alluding to at the time. I thought at that time that my involvement was just simply my knowledge. I was far too busy trying too hard to see the obvious, that thing called too many trees, blocking out the view of the forest. Edith and Anna were only thought of on late sleepless nights.

*Who's Anna? You had not mentioned her before, was she also at the co-sexual prison?*

She was just someone I thought about when I was lonely, a friend that kept me grounded, even though we never crossed that line for some reason. My photographic memory allowed me to put pictures with my sleep therapy and construct a movie to dream by. I would go to my special places and be with whom I needed to be with. That and marijuana kept me sane, calm, and alive.

The next day Half Fast rolled up on me on the south yard. "I need a moment, Bill," he said as I stood arguing prison politics with some of my politically motivated friends. I was eager to hear what he was going to tell me about the event of the day before. So I excused myself at once and strolled along the jogging track, which was what you did if the bleachers did not provide enough seclusion of conversation.

"Bill," he continued as we walked down the ocean side of the track, "it was nearly unfortunate had you of all people been spotted there at that very moment."

"What went down?" I asked methodically. "That looked like the Boyce thing all over again."

"I need you to do something for me," he said in a way that was sincerely honest and straightforward. "This little rat's ass marine with more juices than the first lady just forced me and every other arms dealer in the world to sell him undercover, i.e. illegally, enough weapons to mount war many times for years to come. The worst part is I have to deliver all of it to some of the sickest bastards in the world. Not the people I went into this business to supply. I wish I could tell you more but you already know more than you should ever know but we cannot change that."

"Whatever you need, Shawn, just ask and I will do what I can do!"

"This is not tough, I promise, it just has to be done precisely. After the invoices are filled they are going to cut me loose. That day they are going to roll me up, chain me up, jump suit me, and drag me across the yard so there are enough witnesses to see that nothing is going on out of the norm. When I see you, I will tell you I'm going east if everything is going as planned, west if it's not."

Then he handed me a phone number. "Call it at midnight, tell anyone that answers what I said, and hang up."

"What if I don't see you and I find out later you have been shipped?"

121

"Only if you see me. If you don't see me, do nothing."

"I hope this goes down the way you and your lawyers worked it out."

"Don't give it another thought, Bill. We hold trump on this deal. They try and back up on one item, they fall all the way to the White House. They made themselves dirty for a kick back. I wish I could tell you more but I cannot. Good luck. I hope I never see you again in here!"

As quickly as it all started it was over. Shawn was being hauled from control over to his dorm to pack up. He waved at me from the waist chains and told me he was being shipped east. I made the call at midnight and was told everything was fine and that he was with them now.

Another definition of the term "and for other reasons" my life will never be destined to boredom. It was one of God's Sundays, warm sunshine, a light breeze, and the big money was on a softball game on the south yard that was about to start. I noticed I was pinned by one of the Mexicans that rolled in from Tucson. As soon as I was spotted a runner left for the north yard.

I had just gotten down to the first row of the bleachers to place a small wager on the game. This Mexican walked over in front of me. He was smiling ear to ear when he reached out and put his hand on my shoulder, leaned in close to my left ear, and whispered a message.

"Angel was hit as he got off the bus in Talladega and was stabbed nineteen times before the armed U.S. marshals could pull the assailant off him. Angel is not expected to live. You have been redeemed, my brother."

I hoped he was dead, however I did not feel as if his spirit was gone from this world. It was not the kind of news I wanted on such a splendid day. It was prison and you get what you got, that is an old prison saying. You catch what you pitch, and you do not shit where you eat. These are so much more valuable than the ambiguously stated advice of Old Cape Cod.

# CHAPTER FIFTEEN
# THE THIRD PART, A TIME OF RECKONING!

*Judge Waters was* ordered to rehear my case on the judicial provision of considered false information at time of sentencing. The bottom line to that was Judge Waters could give me the hearing and say no to the release, in which case the Circuit Court would then order him to release me. The time it takes to make that happen is eighteen months. My time left to my mandatory release date was only eight months down the road.

You did not have to be a fortune teller to figure that one out. You just need to understand the term "kangaroo court." They call it that because calling it a "jack asses court" would be disrespectful of the jack asses. The jack asses in black robes, the ones who are being overturned for the sake of justice, is outweighed by their perfect score card. So much for blind justice; she is blindfolded so she does not have to see the whores in black robes who dispense justice as if it were apples and oranges.

*He did not let you out; I've got that. That is not the end of the story. Too much has happened and I still do not know where this journey ends.*

Eight months turned into eighteen months, with another ninety days in the hole. It takes longer to appeal a mandatory release date than it takes to do the whole sentence calendar for calendar. One day while sitting in the law library, my good friend from a prominent sea port city of North Africa—which he scammed for more millions than I could print on a good run—pointed out a passage in *Black's Law*. He was the same individual who pointed out Title 18, USC 1001 (trick and device), the key to locking up every elected, appointed, or hired government employee. Just read it and it will make your heart sing, unless you just happen to be one of them.

From his deep, genetic African voice came words that just sounded so much more important when he spoke them with his rich British accent.

This was not one of those things, it was one of those dark rules that the lawmakers just happen to slip under the Constitution and past our deaf and blind Supreme Republican Court justices as they are naked under their robes.

It read in brief that if the government could fabricate the possibility that if a sophisticated criminal is likely to re-offend after completing his sentence, he could then be held without trial until such time as the government no longer considered him a threat.

I love it when my opponent sets out on a bad trip. Traveling in opposition of the Constitution is not something they want to be caught doing publicly, the reason they brag about Republicanizing the Supreme Court. It is perhaps why I'm compelled to tell my story over and over again. Remember this legal fact: When any member of the government, judiciary or law enforcement violates one single individual's individual rights, they commit treason against everyone else.

*How are you going to beat them when you cannot even get re-sentenced or released on your two-thirds mandatory release date?*

I knew now that this obscure provision was earmarked with my name on it. In my prison jacket was the provision under which they could extend my sentence. Perhaps they hoped my extension would be the final straw my heart needed to end my life for reasons of national security, that dirty rug under which our government hides all of their hideous mistakes.

This mistake will be dubbed: I will not go quietly into the night. I had groomed my job as prison printer so well that I had access to all the tools I needed to foil their little plan.

For some time I had been working in collaboration with the prison shrink. We had three different post-Vietnam syndrome groups at TI where the population was better than 50 percent Vietnam era vets I had taken a survey of my own when I discovered that the Olympics were using Hueys for security and twice a day they would fly dead across the south yard. So I sat in the bleachers and estimated how many men were in my line of sight. Then when the Hueys flew over I counted the number of heads that dipped, or rather the number of heads that did not dip.

We would sit opposing each other in a circle of inmates you would never want to meet, dark night or light of day. Then he would ask a question that no one would respond to. Then I would verbally poke at the hard shell of the inmate until he would come out of his silent world and through snarling teeth you would hear more truth than you want to know, the largest number of teenagers ever sustained in battle for years, under conditions that best support snakes and insects big enough to crack with a baseball bat. The jungle is dark at night, moving is the sound that kills you. It was kind of like prison—you are never safe.

My Boron friend Dave was the shrink's clerk. He showed me the phone ropes and the number I needed to call to reach the head shrink at USC Medical Center. At precisely eleven forty-five I called the number of

Professor Rob White, who at that very moment was in the final stage of a Ph.D. in criminology.

After he identified himself as the head of the department, I started right in with, "How would you like to get into the head of the man who printed over fifteen million dollars in twenties, fifties, and hundreds and was instrumental in Christopher Boyce's escape from Lompoc Maximum Security Prison?"

Without so much as breath of air Professor Rob White said, "Wednesday be okay?"

That was it. He asked no questions so I told him no lies. The next step took me to the office over the mess hall and the man who had kept me off the bus for four months. Now I had another little fix for him to do.

"What do you need today, Killer?" Gregg asked with his big gay smile.

"Put a Doctor Rob White on control's visiting list to do a study on inmate Jennings, pending release psychological examination. Use the regional code in the authorization column."

"This Wednesday?" Gregg asked, pressing the enter key.

I nodded and it was done. My parole jacket stated that before I got released I must have a complete psychological evaluation. I now knew why that was put in my jacket from the get-go. If I did not get a ringer to do it for real the right way and get a true evaluation, then I will be doing life on the short track.

If a prison shrink did my evaluation then they would come up with the answer the government wanted, just like the way they handle Social Security disability. All Social Security doctors owe the government and violating the Hippocratic Oath is how they demand payment. Student loans, taxes, or the misuse of a controlled substance. The government will destroy any integrity one might have for fear of prison. That was the Republican Congress's sure-fire plan to slow the growth of Social Security disability, the Congress that saw no medicinal value for marijuana, like they find in nicotine, alcohol, and silicone breast implants. After all, marijuana never killed anyone like nicotine kills those who never smoked and alcohol kills people who never drank a beer on spring break as a minor.

*What will happen to you when they figure out what you did?*

At that point, the only thing I knew was I had the dream three times, when they kept me in the navy past my discharge date. That happened and now I had dreamt three times that they are going to keep me past my release date. The stakes were high and that was when my game peaked. Whether they caught it now or later, I got the ace in my shoe that goes with the three in my hand. I was never comfortable with the label the government hung on my jacket, "conman and manipulator." It's not a con, it's a scam. A con is built on lies, the scam is based in truth.

When Wednesday afternoon rolled around, I had forgotten what day it was and took a nooner joint for a stroll around the park. When I was walking to the stroll my name was broadcast all over the compound, shaking me back to the reality of prison.

David met me on the Freeway. "Are you stoned? What were you thinking? How are you going to scam this shrink when you reek of some really good shit? Are you going to share any of that with me?"

"This is just our get-acquainted meeting. I'm not flying any flags until he comes back for a session. Give me a mint and a squirt of your stinky water," I said, flagging him off and popping two-thirds of a joint into his shirt pocket.

As it turned out, no one questioned anything, except the question Dr. Rob White put to me: "What do you want out of this?" he asked.

I looked at him with a *what do you mean by that?* look on my face.

"I know what the government wants to find out although I do not know why they need to know. I just think that you should get something out of it. So I ask you again, what would you like to prove or find out about yourself?"

"Well, sure I'd like to know whether or not I'm paranoid or are they out to get me and if so, why?"

Dr. Rob White, with his buff-colored skin and the distinctively black wavy hair that made him appear obviously not comfortable with his racial origin, said, "Fair enough, Mr. Jennings, I will make it a point to determine paranoia or not. I will be coming here two to three times a week for six weeks and testing you in a number of ways to determine your strength and weaknesses, your mental stability, and how you relate to your surroundings. Do you agree to this study and will you honestly participate in the process? Are you doing this of your own free will?"

"Yeah, I'll give you my best shot. I just hope that your findings and opinions will be based only on what transpires between the two of us, that no one interferes or influences your determinations."

Robby took facial concern with the steady even tone of my words and the fact that I locked up his eyes until I was finished.

"I am a doctor and you are legally my patient, not the Federal Bureau of Prisons. I am not naïve, Mr. Jennings. I understand why the government wants me to do this study. However, let me assure you I have my own agenda, as I am doing my final semester for a Ph.D. in criminology. You have already demonstrated that you are of above-average intelligence; I will be measuring just how intelligent you are. We have a number of mathematical tests that will determine your ability to solve problems. Do you like math, Mr. Jennings?"

"I was never any good at math until all of the apples and oranges were gone, and they introduced me to the dollar signs. Then suddenly everything made sense, when I discovered the math of building things." Then I stopped, realizing I was too high to be talking about me and I stopped. Besides he was already hooked and he had not set up his tape recorder yet. He had that petrified fear in his face that he would not remember exactly what I said. I was impressed that he was aware that the order of spontaneous conversation was the key to understanding one's intent and that equates to one's level of thinking. I was a consummate salesman. I opened, I closed, and now the dance would begin. At this point in time, I only had a vague idea as to what it was I needed to create out of this evaluation.

Out on the yard it was business as usual. The Jewish lawsuit and the Mexican food rights lawsuit proved that diet changes constituted cruel and unusual punishment. Then there were the Native American issues. Native Americans should be at the front of every line for government benefits. Put yourself in these shoes: you are a reservation Native American, Vietnam vet with a federal beef. Where is that line, or are the white eyes of our government still viewing them as savages? Is that why it was okay to just take everything, including their culture, and make them the longest prisoner of war victims in history. They did not believe in the same way as the white man. I am proud of what my Native American brother has achieved and what they will make from it.

During all of this, I was trying to recover embezzled "good time" from my first three joints, thanks to Peter Avillinoza and his grudge match tampering.

I was feeding Rob paperwork from my jacket and he was nervously accepting it. My friend David had read the original handwritten draft of *Pressed for Time* and said as he caught up with me on my stride from the south yard to the north compound, "Don't let them find out how smart you are or they will never let you go."

I had been aware that nearly every test exercise he gave me had only one purpose—that was to determine my IQ. He allowed me to take his marking pen to trace images that had never been documented before in his hundred-year-old ink spot book. Then he could not wait to leave so he could share this new image with his colleagues. He would show me a picture then ask me to tell him a story about the picture. I told him three different stories about each picture until I got bored.

He had a book that was full of number games. I flew through it as fast as he could turn the pages. When I would see the last few pages of a section I would just quit. David was right—I had never thought that I was a geek. This was not the first time I was tested. I took my first Iowa Standard Aptitude Test in the third grade. I had not received a passing grade and they could not figure why. Then I aced the SAT; that really confused the school and they confused my parents. By the time I got to the fifth grade, I still had not received a passing grade and once again, I aced the SAT, answering 100 percent of the questions and scoring 98 percent. The part they could not figure out was I did not have the reading skills to read more than 10 percent of the questions in the time allotted. So they packed me up and sent me to Boston University to be tested and studied.

They read me the test, and I scored four grades higher than the one I was in. You see, I was the youngest. My sister and brothers were two, seven, and ten grades ahead of me.

Both my mother and father were well read and well spoken. I had a college level vocabulary but I could not read or spell the words I knew how to use effectively in conversation. A gift and a curse—imagine being a perfect writer and you had nothing to write. I had ideas too great to describe with the words I could spell. I easily accepted the theory of the school principal that I was a slow learner, I was lazy, and did not try hard enough.

However in 1956 or 1957, Henry Shaw the principal of Governor John Carver School, sent a document to the FBI reporting that I had a genius IQ and that I was a non-conformist, a fact he was more than aware of by then.

By the time I was tested for the navy, I had already answered and discussed every answer in every test that was being used by everyone at that time. As a failing high school sophomore, I scored the eleventh highest score of the Eleventh Naval District, in 1962.

This is what our FBI was doing after World War Two, because they knew Hitler was a genius and a non-conformist, that he had light-colored hair and blue eyes. I also had blue eyes and light color hair. Did they just label me at age thirteen or create me?

*You scored 98 percent of 100 percent of the questions and you could only read 10 percent of the questions. When they read you every question, you only scored four grades higher than your grade level. How do you explain that?*

It is simple—I cheated. When I was in the third grade, I discovered a re-occurring pattern to the marks on the answer sheet. Soon after that, I discovered that by answering about ten questions of every hundred, I had enough time to do the entire section before the time's up bell would ring. The indignant man from the Iowa Institute, who claimed loudly that there was no pattern to the answers, after a simple demonstration proved him to be wrong on all five tests when I scored 98 percent. The indignant man said, "See, he is not a genius—he cheated." Then he ran out of the room before my dad could backhand the little pencil neck geek.

It was not until the study was almost completed when they realized they had all been dancing to my music. Dr. Rob did not like being in the middle of a sting that was not of the government. Warden Richard Risen was angry about finding out I tripped him up again. A Mormon warden, every inmate that got to work on the warden's house got a lesson in polygamy from the hot, sexy, sensual Mormon wife. They were bound and determined to make all of this work for them. The flaw in their plan was it was not their plan.

A good scam is built of truth and like everyone always said, the truth will set you free. One day Fat Smith was escorting me back from the hole when he said I should stop fighting the system.

I told Fat Smith the biggest mistake the feds would make would be to let me out of the federal prison system alive. He looked at me with disbelief or total confusion; with Smith it was hard to tell. For me I had to treat it like all gut feelings, you have them for a reason. I have a logical mind and contrary to what people might think, all my decisions are the result of speculating over the known relevant information. All of that added up to the undeniable fact that the feds would be better off if I was dead, and everything I wrote down and sent out just disappeared. One was not an option without the other. That is why I wrote a lot of things down and sent them to a lot of different people.

The study was finally over. There were no more IQ tests left anywhere in California. Doctor Rob was reluctant to conclude this relationship. He informed me that the next time he came, he would have his complete report of my evaluation, that I should not be concerned, as it was highly favorable and not open to collateral attack. "I think you understand the legal meaning behind that," he said as he shook my hand and departed.

Meanwhile I was working the numbers to get out before the fourth of July 1985. There was just too much unapplied good time. When I busted Avillinoza, it triggered a flurry take downs of other crooked compound cops. TI was the place where just about anything from furloughs and meritorious good time to early releases was traded for expensive cars and vacations in places they cannot afford on cop pay. Seldom was it cash. Cash has no tracks, but the other things left tracks back to the giver so the receiver could not back out of the deal. Thanks to Peter ratting out everyone else just to catch a break, TI staff was non-responsive to reinstatement of the good time that Avillinoza embezzled from my records. The regional office in Burlingame had even less sympathy for my plight until I took a stroll in the shit pond for a thirty-day meritorious good time award. This was the first time ever for performing that service good time was not awarded.

Then one day the good doctor returned with his report. As he handed the seventeen-page evaluation to me he added, "Mr. Jennings, to your question as to paranoia, you are not paranoid. There are those out there that are out to get you and I do not know why, and I am sorry."

I was told I could read it, however I could not make copies or take notes. I looked at the good doctor and laughed lightly. The doctor had to know that just by looking at it, I had my copy.

*Without a copy you cannot prove that the report existed. It will be your word against theirs.*

The first paragraph started out with basic information: Mr. Jennings is not paranoid, nor does he demonstrate any threatening behavioral tendency, nor is he likely to re-offend once he is released from custody.

Mr. Jennings has a highly pragmatic mind, with an IQ much greater than 135. "Rob," I said, "how much greater than 135? Are we talking 5 points, 10 points, what?"

Rob's nervous look turned to one of hostility when he turned to face me. "It is just a number. It does not mean anything. It's just a number. It is not important!"

"You give me every IQ test known to man three times a week for six weeks just to get a number that does not mean anything?"

"Jennings, please just read the report and sign off on it so I can go and put this all behind me."

"The government already has a copy," I asked, trying to figure out this total change in his otherwise gratuitous behavior.

The report stated that I was in excellent mental health, especially considering the circumstances of my incarceration that was meant to be taken at face value. I looked at the doctor and he nodded, as he knew where I was in the report.

He drove his fist into his open hand and ground it in, then he took both hands and placed them over his eyes, rubbing them deeply. "I am sorry, Jennings, but this is the best I could do in protecting this study. They know you are going to try to use this study to get yourself out of prison."

I scanned the information I expected to be there and freeze-framed words, sentences, and paragraphs that were definitive. Thankfully, I had six weeks to hone my skills and be graded as I went along, day by day. It was so easy for me to do this now that Doctor White asked me several times if I was sure I had read the entire thing.

The very moment Rob left, I used the phone right there in the shrink's office to call my USC law student.

"You have to give me word for word those things that will demonstrate your right to hold a copy," Larry asked with so much excitement I was sure that the red-haired freckled-faced young wannabe lawyer's face was flashing like a traffic signal.

After I gave him ten times more than he needed, he assured me that an injunction would be filed before the close of court that day.

I knew he had not lied as I was scooped up off of the yard and thrown in the hole. It was me, they did not need a reason. They could always make something up later. The stupid idiots did it on the night I had a visit with the law students. Two days later the law student had a copy of the report and a court-order releasing me from the hole.

This incident threatened the little fifteen thousand dollar grant the prison system was paying the university. If they had followed my lead I would have gotten them to increase it by at least one more zero. They were also ordered to never have contact or discuss this information with me ever again in life. The government gets a lot more for themselves for my money than I can get for myself with my money.

Then one day it happened. I was on my way to lunch when I was paged to the warden's office. I had a hammer-sized joint ready to smoke after lunch, so I dropped it in a safe spot and proceeded to the warden's office. No one was in sight, as the door stood open a few inches. I knocked with the intent to swing the door all the way open so I would not walk in on a dead body.

I saw Dr. Rob White standing in front of the warden's desk; no one else was present in the room as I looked behind the door when I entered.

"Come in, William," Dr. White beckoned me with his words and his hand. "Please close the door behind you," he said, looking down at the floor as he paced nervously. "The court has ordered me to tell you what we set your IQ at. However before I do that the institution told me to warn you that if you do not stop using the evaluation to try and get out of prison, they will just order me to change it."

"Fine, change one word and I will be out of here in forty-eight hours. So now, tell me what you have been ordered to tell me."

"We estimate your IQ to be around 210, however as you withdrew on many of the complex tests we feel that you chose how high you were willing to let us test you. I was angry about that, however now I understand why you did this. You just wanted to prove that you were fit for release and I did not understand that you did not want them to find out just how mentally agile you seem to be. We also understand why the government wants to know how much you could or would understand from the magnitude of the events you have knowledge of. The other thing that the feds are concerned with is the level of sophistication of your printing operation. They still believe that you had access to the original artwork.

"You tricked me and used me. I was getting this Ph.D. so I could work for the federal government as an expert witness. That is pretty much out of the question now."

I pretty much lost interest in what he had to say after the words of "around two hundred and ten." *Slow learner, did not catch on, lazy, does not apply himself.* I went to the phone to call my mother and find out something for myself.

I asked when it was that they knew I had a genius IQ. They had thought so in the fifth grade, however after sending me to BU when I was in the seventh grade, they were sure. Then I asked why I was never told. Her answer was what I expected: Henry Shaw said that if I was told, it would just make me lazy. I did not fault my mother, as she was of the generation that trusted authority. She was sure they knew best. Henry Shaw knew I was a non-conformist and that made me evil in that day of ignorance and fear.

I was just beginning to understand the potential of the gifts I had. It was like I had just been given a brand new toy that came to me without instructions. I would play with it until I understood how to push all of the buttons to make it fully functional. I had to think about how I would use what I had. For the first time, my plan had little to do with money and more to do with manifesting what I would become now that I understood that my ideas were not ludicrous. The problem was that others could not see what was obvious to me at a glance. Every illogical problem has a logical answer. Questions are the route to the solution. We can fly through space on the magnetic waves and currents in space without rockets or fuel. Energy greater than any rocket or engine exists all around us and is in everything. Knowing that does not make me special, but being capable of figuring out how to plug into all that energy does.

I needed to get on with my life. I needed to discover what I was created with the ability to do and get on with it. It was time for me to leave prison and spend as long as it took to discover the real me. I had been hiding too long as a lazy, slow learner. It was a mask that never felt right even though I had bought into it for the better part of forty years.

The feds were realizing that the dirty shuffle was not going to work on me. I think it was then I told my case manager that the biggest mistake the feds were going to make was letting me out alive. I did not know for sure at that time why I was compelled to say it again.

"What are you going to do, Jennings?" he asked like my life did not matter.

So I gave him an answer he would never understand. "One of two things," I said. "I will either learn the rules to the game better than the game maker himself or I will change some of the rules to the game and not tell them until after I win." I loved doing that to people who think they are smart because they work for the government. I am an outlaw, I work for myself. I do not do another man's bidding for a paycheck. It seemed to me that if I could create an economy for myself in prison that was greater than my pay of thirty-four cents an hour, then I would have no problem creating a lifestyle that would allow for my free expression of myself, to create all of the things I have created in my mind. I would now be able to make real, like the vertical hydraulic accelerator, the electric magnetic looped system. Combustible fuel would have no purpose in a logical world. Fossil petroleum being converted into air pollution is an ignorant use for such an exhaustible reserve.

If you pick up a 1937 encyclopedia and read what was known about solar energy, you would have to ask yourself why did we build nuclear power plants. You probably will not like the answer you come up with. Some day soon you will see the absurdity of manufacturing and transporting electricity and your grandchildren will ask why.

Then, as if there had never been a problem, I was to be released at six A.M. on the third of July 1985. David came by to see me on my last day. David had been a secret agent with the NIS, and he still had friends who would drop off a word to him from time to time.

"Bill," he said, after we entered his room and shut the door, "I am glad you are getting out of here and going to the street. They are going to try and take you out from the bow of one of the ships in the yard across from the release gate. You are going to have to figure out how you are going to get from the sally gate to the coffee wagon. If you make it to the roachcoach you will be able to use the pay phone to call a cab. Here is the number, ask for Freddie. Freddie will take you where you want to go and smoke you up on the way."

I had already given a lot of thought about the possibility that if they wanted to hit me, that would be the time. Then they could claim that it was a mob hit and nobody would give it a second thought. Then of course there were all of those copies of my story, *Pressed for Time*, written before I understood what really went on while I was breaking the law, printing money, and doing time.

That morning I gave all of my shit away to those I would be leaving behind. All I took was the clothes I was wearing and one well-packed box of the paperwork of the last five and a half years, along with the hardcover file folders. Standing all of my legal work on edge, it provided a solid ammo blocker. Carrying the box on my left shoulder would block out my entire kill zone from the angle from which my assailant would be targeting me from if I walked down the middle of the narrow street.

If they could not get an instant guarantee one-shot kill, they would not take a shot. David told me so. As I started down the narrow street lined with high chainlink fence on both the prison and the shipyard side, I did see one hooded man scampering around the bow of one of the smaller ships that were with the bow toward the street. My next glimpse of the man, I saw him crouched down and leaving the bow with his laser scoped rifle. I dashed the last few yards to the coffee truck. The first call I made was to Diane. All I said was, "I am out." The next call was to Yellow Cab. Before I could say anymore the dispatcher announced that he was sending Freddie. Freddie took me to the Rocket Club in the little city of Lenex.

# CHAPTER SIXTEEN
# HOME FREE!

*After touching base* with Big Mac, I was off to the airport in Mac's limo. Going back to Diane was not going to work. It seemed that it did matter, Diane being with someone else did matter. That was not the reason we fought; we created other reasons to fight about. However this time the hostilities did not end with sex. It ended by me driving Diane away and back into the arms of her lover.

*What was it like being out in the free world after five and half years locked up?*

The very first day was the fourth of July, and of course that meant a rush trip to the store. I remember it like it just happened yesterday. Me, Diane, and Sonya had just pushed our cart into the check-out line. Suddenly they thought of two items they had forgotten. Diane went off in one direction and Sonya went off in the other. I was left standing in line with the cart. Then this sneaky idiot with two packs of hot dog buns and no cart does a dodge, weave, and ends up in front of me in line.

I flashed back to prison law. This slimy little wimpy bastard just told everyone by his action that I was a punk. It all happened so fast, the next thing I knew I had him pinned to the candy rack by his neck. With my voice so loud it rattled the windows I yelled, "What the FUCK! You did not see me standing there?" At that point, I looked up and time stopped. No one was moving; everyone was frozen in mid-stride. Diane was to my left and Sonya to my right. Our eyes locked and then Sonya bolted for the door on her side and Diane was dashing through the door at her end. I released the man and bolted out as Diane was already backed out and Sonya was holding the rear slider door open. That was exciting but I did not go out much after that. It took a long time to adjust to a totally different value system. The less you have of possessions the more value you put on the nontangibles.

After five and a half years of living, breathing, and fighting the feds tooth and nail, just to be with the most fantastic match for the child in me, it was over. Diane was my dream girl that my friends ribbed me about when

I was just a kid growing up in Carver. I had a dream three times. I was walking through a young stand of pine trees. The girl I had my arm around, I could not see what her whole face looked like but I knew I loved her more than anyone.

We never knew that the little bad girl from Ohio and the little bad boy from Massachusetts would meet and fall in love in California. It was over, at least for now. I packed my stuff and with nothing, not even my dignity, with me blaming her and her blaming me, I left. In retrospect, one might see that to complete this journey I needed to be on my own and set my own course.

My ex-wife, after refusing to allow my children to visit me in prison for all of the wrong reasons for over five years, now had it rigged that if I came near them I would be arrested and thrown back in prison. That added to the anger within me. My ex was probably right—I could very well kill her. However killing someone who has made a habit out of threatening to take their own life is not logical if the murder is for revenge.

*You have such a cold heart after being in prison. She is still the mother of your children. That should pardon her for anything she may have done to you.*

I was not angry with her for what she had done to me. My anger was for the unnecessary scars she inflicted on our children that she in time would pay for through her own means. Knowing that is solace for my pain now. I have survived prison against great odds, the street holds no fear for me.

Visiting with my parents was tough. At forty, I was still the child and I had been bad. However it was my father who set me straight on things again. "Your mother was on her knees every night for hours praying for you, sometimes until her knees would bleed. I just thought you should know that," he said then walked away, leaving me to consider his words in the shade of my uncle's castor bean tree.

That knocked my ego down a notch. After thinking that it was my quick glib tongue and my ability to outmanipulate the feds on their own turf, I suddenly realized that it was my mother pulling at the robe of Jesus that gave me the edge that allowed me to stay on top of my game.

*Throughout your story, you demonstrate a strong Christian belief which seems to contradict your life style choices. How does a person with a 210 IQ and a logical, pragmatic mind nurture a belief in God?*

God, for me, is the most logical concept man has projected, although my concept of God is most likely significantly different from most people's concept of God, the creation of the earth and of humankind. For instance, how can you look into the face of a multi-racial child and not understand what the image of God really means, but still you ask the question. You argue about ideas that you have defined by words, creation, evolution, everlasting, but most of all forgiveness! I read the whole Bible; I saw only three basic rules.

Love, live life abundantly, and if you screw up, ask to be forgiven. Why do you think God gave us such a great guarantee for life everlasting?

Just think how great life would be if they had allowed Social Security to give us all a guarantee of financial security after being a taxpayer all of our adult lives, through the creation of the Social Security bank of the people. We could then be free to pursue our dreams any way we chose. Win or lose, when you stop working, you will reap the dividend of the commerce you help to create. It sounds fair because it is logical.

I was out on the street. I had no one in my life, and after eighteen months of screwing everything with two legs and tits I finally settled into a nice two-bedroom mobile home, got myself a baby blue Pontiac Grand Prix, and started living for me and seeing my children as much as possible.

The Iran-Contra gun deal was unbelievable the way it was being fed to the people. If you wanted to know the truth all you had to do was wait six to eight weeks and Reagan would contradict his earlier statement.

If you want to know the definition of national security, it is the unspoken truth, making it by definition the greatest lie ever told. Understanding that pretty well defines the Reagan/Bush regime. They had more secrets in those twelve years then I did in five and a half years in federal prison.

While I was still in the joint at TI, I heard and saw President Ronald Reagan make a statement that I have heard only other criminals make. Reagan said, "They can't prove we broke the law." That has a totally different meaning than "we did not break the law" but no one lit him up for that. Not then, and not later.

*You really seem to hate everything about this country.*

Quite the contrary, you will find no greater patriots than those you meet in federal prison. Believe me, I was as shocked as anyone to discover patriotism in a federal prison system that held a national level of over 50 percent Vietnam and Korean war veterans.

Finding out that Ronald Reagan was asking how long it would take to be ready for a major military involvement in the Gulf while he was arming Saddam Hussein with weapons of mass destruction is just a little too discerning at the time he was doing it. In retrospect, it is incriminating, aiding in the theatrics of war to feign a supportive justification for aggression.

We change our leaders every four years as we continue to live under a dictatorship of laws. This is not what we were given; it is, however, what we inherited. How can there be a right to life, when we cannot choose when it is time for you to die? Yet we can be drafted into war by those laws and be killed before our time.

Liberty, the right to move about at will, turned into carrying cards with numbers, pictures, and soon DNA.

You will agree to all of this because they never told you the definition of the pursuit of happiness, when back in the day happiness stood for safety, security, and the pursuit of same. Once achieved, happiness is knowing you are safe and secure.

So why do our leaders spend all of our money and so much of their time making us feel unsafe and insecure? Constantly attacking every age group with problems, the government created for them with rules they must obey and a national debt that you must pay. Even before you are born the government, under law, harnesses you more than it makes you free.

It is way past the time for the people to take back our government as we are instructed to do in the preamble of the Declaration of Independence.

It is the only thing our founding documents require the citizen to do in exchange for our constitutional right! That single right that guarantees that this servant government obeys the instruction for the operation and maintenance of the people's government. The word is "abolish." It stands alone as if self-defining.

I would propose that it comes down to: Are we turkeys swallowing rain or are we eagles soaring free on our own wings? Humankind was created self-sufficient. It is a leadership government that requires us to be dependant.

However, without us the government has no power or authority, according to our founding documents. Take that into consideration the next time you cast your vote for either a leader or a public servant.

That should leave you with only one question: What is the difference between a leader and a dictator? The leaders are all in the military and the dictator is in the White House!

*I am sorry; you are going to have to do better than some general allegation and jailhouse platitudes to convince me that thing are as you claim.*

Fine, then let us do a little history review. Let us go back for just a second to the Nixon-Watergate fiasco. When the government wants you to forget about something they cram you so full of crap that in time you forget the principal reason and justification of the act.

Was there information of the nature Nixon alleged or was he lead to believe there was information that the Democrats would use in the election about stuff he knew would incriminate him of something that he already had to know he was guilty of?

*Are you going to tell us what it was about because we know what they claimed had nothing to do with the truth.*

Actually, the only thing that is relevant to this example is what happened as a result of Nixon being busted. Obviously, that was the end product the choreographer was striving to accomplish. Otherwise, Nixon would have claimed national security to justify his act. However, then there would have to be some national security violation he could have pinned on the Democrats just before a national election.

As none of that happened, then the end result was the desired result as only the Republican Party could have benefited from his quick dismissal and the replacement of him by a non-threatening individual. One quick sweep and the dirt was gone, leaving a clean slate for the election.

*I do not get it. We still do not know what Watergate was about.*

That's what we call dodging the bullet. When I took my first and last college history course, I was introduced to an insightful concept of history. The history professor said on the first day, "Those of you who have gone through school getting A's in history because you can spell everyone's name right and you memorized all the dates when people were born, served, signed stuff, and died, you people are not going to do well in my course. That is not what history is about, or our reason for studying it. History is about events and what happened as a result of those events. You are going to have to think, to recreate everything the way it was, to understand why things happened the way they did. You will find out in time that history does not happen in an intellectual world, it is created."

The event, and then what happened? How did the government react, how did it change things for the economy, the people, and the government? What was done or what happened as a result of the event? Sometimes it is hard to believe that what seems like a non-related event changes or alters history from what should have happened into something quite different.

When the government wants to find and identify the ringleader of a conspiracy, it creates a copability scale, identifying which person is the most essential person in the conspiracy. I will now prove all of my earlier allegations about Reagan, Bush, Oliver North, and Bush Jr. using the same test they use to lock up all of us disgruntled Vietnam vets.

*You are going to prove that they wagged the dog?*

The result of a created event becomes the motive. So the test is quite simple even though all of the political ringsiders cannot see the fire because of all the smoke. Those people may not have wagged the dog, however they were undeniably scratching it behind the ears.

The answer that Reagan got was ten years, and guess who was in the White House in ten years. George Bush, the ex-CIA director and the last vice president. Sounds like a person who had authority over the government personnel necessary to choreograph and orchestrate everything, including the procurement of "my" entire counterfeit operation.

While Congress was dragging their feet on a twenty million dollar package of military aid to Central America, someone with authority to do so released evidence from a court holding room and rolled over ten million dollars of my counterfeit money three times.

*How does the government roll ten million in counterfeit over three times and why?*

Number one, they needed to purchase a lot of weaponry. More than twenty million, more than fifty million. There were other sources as well, petroleum kicked down, and of course the people who manufacture the tools of war threw in what I am sure they considered it to be seed money. There are other countries as well; it was called a guaranteed annuity. You can count the players by the brand names of the enemy's toys.

How much do you suppose a decade-old aircraft is worth on the black market, even with the latest upgrades? However you could give it away and then sell the U.S. government ten brand new state of the art fighter aircraft to shoot it down some time in the future.

When counterfeit is recovered from other countries, by the Secret Service, the U.S. treasury pays 100 percent on the dollar for it, that's the law. It is like having a check you can write again and again if you are a leadership government.

When you do business with outlaws, you must take a cut or you are not really in. So Oliver North got caught sitting on a sizeable Swiss account, considering his annual income.

Everything was right on schedule. Saddam Hussein had gone from friend to archenemy just in time to bring the president to a just and moral decision to attack the evil empire. Ten years goes by fast when you are on the street and nobody but the Republicans were in the White House, the same major players for twelve years!

Ronald Reagan tripled the national debt and created out-of-control inflation. He claimed to be railroaded by the tax-and-spend Democrats. However he spoke a sentence and his words brought the wall down. Amazing how he controls another country's evil leader but his own Congress was out of control. Leadership or liership?

Then Bush took control of a crumbling economy and shoved it over the edge by going to war with a man who was a threat to our freedom, national security, and the world.

I was baffled, as we were still pissed over Vietnam, how well the spin doctors were able to create a Star Wars enthusiasm for this conflict. It was so well done that people who spoke out against the war were shamed for not supporting the troops who had gone off to secure safety for us scared, timid America and secure our freedom abroad.

That was when the mentality was born to support your president in time of war or you are a bad American. Peer pressure instead of mass beatings in the street to stifle decanters. They had found that did not work in the sixties.

I think it is important to understand that while the feds were redefining privacy, organized crime was redesigning their world as well. The CEOs were the new age godfathers and the CEO holds Ph.D.s in whatever is necessary to put a corporate shield around high-tech enterprise. They were now clean enough to associate quite publicly with people in high places in the government. Those who played ball with the fed were protected by the fed. Those who would not provide government access to every PC they manufactured would be prosecuted for not providing an even playing field for his competitors, making it against the law to build a better machine. So much for free enterprise that does not serve the leadership agenda.

The Republicans were now the head of organized business and the new business was rifling the abundant economy, bilking trillions from and through the fluff-and-stuff financial reporting of income and profits. Anderson was the underwriter for Corporate Republican fraud at a level that represented more than thirty-two percent of this nation's GNP. Of course, they needed a Republican in the White House to create an economic downfall so the major players could pillage their empires and run down the paper path Cheney wrote and cashed in on it first so he could finish the process as the voice behind the throne. Everyone else had to wait until our financial downfall was signed (liquidation of our federal reserves), sealed (the tax cut), delivered (on September eleventh in New York and the Pentagon), sealed our economic doom. Failure for profits that started back in the Reagan regime trickled down to this.

If you could go back and change history, you would only have to change the Supreme Court's decision that made Bush President. How different would the world be today if the national guard had been ordered in to re-poll the entire state?

Back in the days of deregulation followed by re-regulation, some bankers who were dirty went to prison camp, and some were granted the too-stupid-to-know-what-was-going on clause.

Just a few years later younger Bush became this genius investor and made big bucks in a football buy-and-sell scam that was so obvious the IRS did not pop to what it really was—a political contribution with a tax cut on both ends of the deal. It is what the younger Bush defined as a win-win situation.

After eight years of the best economy ever in the United States, the lowest unemployment at nearly no inflation as the national debt was being paid down for the first time in debt history, nearly doing away with the minimum pay category and welfare.

Everybody in the Middle East was smiling and shaking hands. In fact things were so good that they had to turn a gentleman's denial into an indictable offense.

What I could not figure out was whatever gave the media an idea that they had the right to ask the question? President or not, my bowel movements and my sexual behavior is not the business of this nation, no matter where I move my bowels or indulge in oral relief. Both Bushes lied, falsified, and created false documents and information for the purpose of justifying a war.

To quote a stupid country song, before you start preaching about our freedom and keeping safe this ground we are living on, remember this, my friend: It was Bin Laden who attacked us on that day, not Hussein.

War is for idiots; anyone who is not an idiot knows that already. War produces only losers. In addition, the world threat that we went after was beaten down on his own turf twice in less than thirty days. The only weapons of mass destruction were manufactured and dispensed by George Bush. The terrorist threat is the same as it has always been our entire life. Presidents like the Bush family create the reasons for treason. Before you tell me how terrible Saddam is, let me ask you if you remember this my friend: Kent State, the campus of Berkley, Wounded Knee, Ruby Ridge, and the religious war at Waco, Texas?

How quickly Janet knew why the bombing of Oklahoma City was for the treason committed at Waco. If they had obeyed the Constitution, Waco and Oklahoma would not be a shameful and sad memory.

They took time out to plant my counterfeit money on a deal they called the "Menna Connection." Knowing the back-biting that goes on between the Democrats and the Republicans, I have to wonder how Clinton as a Democratic governor got his hands on my box with my money banded with rubber bands the way I only did so. Just watch the video Rush sold as proof Clinton was dirty. Looks like the chicken coop has a skunk in it, Rush!

No matter how many times Janet Reno tells the lie, they were there as a military force to kill. They were there to make sure that all the munitions and arms sold to David by ATF agents were all present and accounted for. Other than the manner the weapons and munitions were sold to David by the ATF, I am not aware of any other federal legalities.

To constitute entrapment for the purposed moral justification of violating separation of church and state with deadly precedence, nobody has been allowed to mourn for Waco until just recently. The truth died and was consumed in flames; one needs only your faith in God to know those people did not receive justice.

The death penalty count in Texas should be expanded to include the unlawful execution of all those men, women, and children. Being a religious fanatic should not justify execution without a trial for the entire congregation.

As Janet Reno is void of any moral character, never realizing that someone might be appalled, she justified her military massacre of provoked and threatened citizens with the other death sentence nametag, "A cult!" She stated later that she grieves. I grieve too, because she still breathes and lives well on your tax dollars.

Disgruntled is another word that justifies the killing and incarceration of people in the midst of all this freedom our boys go off to wars in other nations to protect. How many times do they have to tell such an absurd lie before even the mushroom Americans figure out that freedom was won here, and to take it away some nation will have to come here to take it away. Nothing but fear took away anyone's freedom on 9/11. Free people should not surrender their freedom so easily. The only freedoms that we no longer have were suspended by order of our imposed leader.

Let me tell you what else I remember. On our way to Vietnam early in the sixties they sang us the same love song. We were going over there so our mommies, daddies, sisters, brothers, and sweethearts would be safe once we freed some people who were being mistreated by their leader. I knew that was far-fetched even for a high school dropout to believe. I was eighteen at the time. Hell, I did not care, I just wanted to blow stuff up and have a lot of sex with a great variety of beautiful Asian women. What did you believe in then compared to what you believe in today?

*How does Waco fit into Iran-Contra, 9/11, Iraq, Bin Laden, and Saddam Hussein?*

Waco: prayer banned in school. God is legal in school only in the Pledge of Allegiance, fear, and bad economic conditions make for a dictate-able con-stitute, just in time for the new president to announce that he wished this was a dictatorship, then he laughed as if it were a joke.

Bush was now on the heels of the evil terrorist and established a nation-al federal police force, which is the first step of every dictator. Destroying the airline business with his knee-jerk reactions, which did not change our vul-nerability to attack by terrorists, the new chief of federal police daily graced our televisions and said words that sounded like, "Now more than ever we need spies in every community" to report anyone who dares to disagree with the Bush regime. Meanwhile every private investor from the Clinton haydays were flat broke and too late to start over for most boomers.

This is not where it started for Bush Jr. He and I go back to when they first decided to clean him up and get him ready for politics. They sat him on the corner of a desk and using my counterfeit money along with the plates and negatives to begin every episode of the TV show about the files of the Secret Service. For that, they paid me zip.

What that proved was the counterfeit money was still in the control of the Republicans, not the Democrats. They attempted to frame Clinton with their drug deals that were the residue of the gun deal. Rebels need money and the U.S. criminalized marijuana, created a source of income when they started flying it in on U.S. government aircraft. Movie directors do not just make that shit up. They just do re-enactments using people who actually have personalities. Now you know why the government knows drugs can pay for trouble.

Then one day this government drone thought he would rip off a few pounds out of every shipment and get rich on the side. What went wrong was it was a government operation that meant everyone was stealing. Everyone tried to frame everyone else. Then they got the good idea to dump it all on Clinton but when that failed, they arranged for a little knee whore from California to give him impeachable sex.

Lying about sex to protect one's personal integrity or lying about war to protect your personal wealth, which is not proper? Which one concerns the American voter the most? That is right—it is immoral to lie when you are asked about receiving oral gratification from an attractive young woman that is not your wife. Somehow that does not match up to the real morality of the age, time, or place where I live, but America bought it through peer manipulation.

No matter how you weigh this catalogue of events, the Republicans are the conspirators and George Bush and his sons are very similar to our enemy. When Florida was a thicket of polling complaints, covering every aspect of the voting process, the Republican Supreme Court, by setting aside the instruction created by our founding documents, they made it about was it was not.

It was not about Gore getting a fair break and it was not about Bush trying to hide the truth about just what it was that little brother promised Daddy he would do to guarantee his big brother the presidency. It was about one single voter that did not get their vote guarantee. It was not just one polling place; it was not just one single polling complaint. Regardless of the number, there was only one legal remedy. It should have been apparent, however nobody seemed to see that elections are not for the candidates. Elections are for the voters; otherwise, it is not a government of the people. That's why criminals own judges and why the Republicans barge about having their judges instead of those liberal Democratic judges that would give everything back to the people. The right answer was to re-vote the whole state. No other remedy guaranteed the promises of every vote. I learned that in the fifth grade. It was not an opinion, it is an instruction of law.

At this time, I think it only fair to point out that Bush to date has kept every one of his campaign promises in record time. The Democrats have never managed to fill every promise but Bush did. He promised to take America in a brand new direction. We were cruising on Rodeo Drive and Bush took us to the dump.

Bush said he was not a peacekeeper, that he would not be a peacekeeper president. Therefore he got his wish for a dictatorship by bankrupting us with a four hundred percent increase in the national debt and antagonizing every small-minded out-dated wannabe world dictator. He has made us broke, scared, and dependent. If he did not do this as a part of a big plan then he is the lamest ass to ever grace the White House.

I cannot wait until the election when Bush blames all of the bad on the Democrats and whatever he thinks is good he will consume all the credit for. The sound bites that they are using today to sell the righteousness of the war, they will use to sell the voter a stupid reason to vote for Bush.

They will expect you to believe that it was only because of Bush leadership that it was possible for the United States to defeat an ignorant dictator. Perhaps he will just postpone the next presidential election for reasons of national security and terrorist threats while he goes after North Korea.

He knows better than all of the other nations of the world. He stood like a punk joiner high school bully and called names of those who would not support his greedy needs. He did so in a manner similar to the way Satan tempted Jesus on the mountain. A person that arrogant will declare himself Supreme Guardian.

You see, when they told Bush he was president, someone said you are now a "world leader." Bush thought that meant he was THE world leader and he threw a hissy fit when everyone did not hunker down before him.

We did not go to war with Saddam Hussein for ten years because anyone ever thought we could not crush him like a bug in an instant. The only safe way to defeat a dictator is to normalize trade and relations. Remember, dictators and those who batter women rule only as long as they are able to sustain poverty, fear, and seclusion. Achieving that in today's world requires a level of seclusion no longer attainable. Bush will remain in the White House as long as the people are willing to submit to created fear and paranoia.

I guarantee Bush will find everything he needs to prove that everything he claimed was justified and more. He will even find documents that prove the connection between Hussein and Bin Laden. However all that money found has a totally different story than Bush will ever admit to.

If this government continues to be an anti-Constitutional leadership government, then I demand that all candidates of the federal government must take college-based SATs and post their scores prior to nomination. You can tolerate a mentally indigent public servant and God knows we have them in abundance. However I damn well know I have a right to the most intelligent and competent leader available, even though someone who is really intelligent will realize that a servant government does not put the people last.

If you were the largest mover and shaker in the United States, what would you have done once Bush announced his plan to improve the economy? You do not rent space and invest in a business when your landlord chooses economic suicide. You want to know why our economy went so quickly in the toilet? It is because the pillars of our economic structure know the basic rule for a good strong economy. A trigger-happy mentally indigent aggressor president who puts the Bush petroleum family of friends first does nothing to provide a farmable sharecropper economy.

You do not send a huge military force to track down a generic-looking man in a desolate country. You do not go deer hunting in an assault vehicle. You do not find a needle in the haystack with a front-end loader. A dozen well-trained personnel could have had him in custody in short order. That is, unless he is in the guesthouse at the Bush ranch. That's where I would have looked on 9/12.

After failing with his big numbers and his big bombs to bring one man to justice, he convinced the mushroom Americans that we needed to save the people under Saddam Hussein to honor the people who were killed on 9/11. He promised to achieve for the people of Iraq that which according to Bush no longer existed in the United States, the right to speak out against their leaders and to have free, unhampered elections.

What is that saying, "What goes around, comes around"? Bush in his infantile mentality changed for everyone the rules of war. From now on, any nation that disagrees with the leadership of another nation can just target the leadership. I think every terrorist should understand that you no longer have to bomb our airports or our financial centers, just target our leadership. Perhaps that, coupled with the dishonorable preemptive failed attack on Iraq leadership, is why all of the intellectual nations in the UN voted against the Bush war. Time will prove that the only thing that Bush liberated was the oil he seized the first day of the war.

All of the treason written against the Constitution was written under a Republican administration. Eradicating a family of herbs from the food chain with an unlawful law—perhaps that is the single cause our culture has so many health disorders. The Supreme Court co-signed Congress medical opinion; the herb known as marijuana and identified as a drug by law enforcement "has no medicinal value." I guess this makes sense to the average IQ.

DCPS, Department of Child Protective Services, AKA, Family Services, authority supercedes the Constitutional protections afforded to the citizens and is abused by a mentally indigent subculture for the purposes of selling children outside the United States and stealing the child's genetic identity for life. Forty years of a 98 percent failure rate.

Family law and juvenile law both extort constitutional safeguards.

Exempting the IRS from conditional law and declaring a war in violation of Geneva convention rules.

Of all of the sins committed against the people, the last one, as a person holding two honorable discharges, Bush has disgraced anyone who has ever depended on those Geneva convention rules for their life. Dictators are the only leaders who hold no regard for the rules of war; I am ashamed that such a man is commander and chief of the people's military.

The same people who condemned the Dixie Chicks for publicly speaking their mind are the same people who did not understand why the people we were liberating did not come running into the streets to welcome the troops. Perhaps the conclusion still evades them. We have become our own enemy! Disagreeing with the war has nothing to do with supporting our troops, this is not a sports event. For a president to hide behind our troops for approval is an evasion of logic. A clearer vision of Bush's cards is what is needed to know his true colors.

The Dixie Chicks did exactly the right thing, in exactly the right place, at exactly the right time. George Bush and his magical spin doctors dodged the bullet that was meant for him and pointed it at the troops. The very next week the polls for the Bush war went up significantly. It had nothing at all to do with the new marriage of ideology, "oppose the war, you oppose the troops." What a spineless leader to not stand and face his decanters on common ground? A commander and chief like that will most likely do what was done to the Vietnam vet. When that went badly they blamed the troops. If this goes badly in a way that the blame-and-punish-seeking Americans can positively identify, who will it be right to blame then? Now that Bush has made the troops the front for his war policies.

My dad, a life-long Republican, asked me one day shortly after Bush was imposed as president, "Do you think he is smart enough to not screw everything up?"

*Suddenly I realized we were right back where we started and without any assistance, the passenger door opened. As I stepped out of the cab on to solid ground, the stranger spoke his final words.*

"I have told you a story about life. What you make of it may very well seal your fate."

*I turned my head against the wind and sand as the old green pick-up truck pulled away. When I looked back the truck was nowhere in sight. The sun was warming the air and a deep blue sky gave new luster to the world around me.*